MW00469931

AMBIENT PARKING LOT

AMBIENT PARKING LOT

PAMELA LU

CHICAGO: KENNING EDITIONS

Kenning Editions
www.kenningeditions.com

Ambient Parking Lot, by Pamela Lu
© 2011 Pamela Lu. All rights reserved.

Portions of this book were previously published in *Antennae*, *Call*,
Chicago Review, *Fascicle*, and *Harper's*.

The premise of this book was inspired by the photograph "Boy Recording
Parking Lot" by New Catalogue (Luke Batten and Jonathan Sadler),
which appeared at Bodybuilder & Sportsman gallery, Chicago, in the
spring of 2003.

The publication of this book has been made possible, in part, by
the generosity of the following donors to Kenning Editions: Charles
Bernstein, Norma Cole, Alan Golding, Lyn Hejinian, Pierre Joris, Kevin
Killian, Hank Lazar, Adalaide Morris, David Pavelich, Susan Schultz,
and Andrea Troolin.

Order from Small Press Distribution
1341 Seventh Street, Berkeley, CA 94710
1-800-869-7553
www.spdbooks.org

Cover design by Brian Grunert, based on a layout by Patrick Durgin.
See: www.whitebicycle.com

Printed on recycled paper.

ACKNOWLEDGMENT

I would like to express my immense appreciation and gratitude to Jennifer Perez—the editor, studio producer, and cocreator of this work—for her dedication to this project. Her vision and intelligence have been instrumental in building and shaping this book into its current form, and I am forever in her debt.

The car has become the carapace, the protective and aggressive shell, of urban and suburban man.

—Marshall McLuhan

Everything in life is somewhere else, and you get there in a car.

—E. B. White

AMPLIFIER

The recording of "Ambient Parking #25" went off without a hitch. Production efforts approached the sublime. We watched in rapture as the parking lot cooperated with our long-arm mike and seemed to relax into the session. The seven-inch vinyl single was released two and a half weeks later on an indie label underwritten by the University of Krakow, with liner notes cribbed from an anonymous dissertation on Hugo Boss:

> The moment is in the line. The line is in the secret. The secret is in the crease. The crease is in the power. The power is in the moment.

Words meant to sketch the condition of high fashion, but which could just as easily be applied to oil-slicked asphalt, acres of grid-striped spaces approximating the breadth and presence of the compact car.

Played back, the music emitted a low earthy growl, privileging bass-level amplitude over quasi-narrative pop disappointment. Stripped down to essentials, the noise had the pounding attitude of reverb without its inbred conservatism. As always, a tough-minded aesthetic kept our minimalist concept intact, while the lusciousness of the infinite loop made even the shoegazers smile. With just a little filtering, the empty landscape managed to express its industrially generated solipsism and came to

3

overshadow even the engine gunning and trunk popping of SUVs.

It was a watershed moment in our recording career. The success of "Ambient Parking #25" buoyed our spirits and encouraged us to reconsider our earlier failures among "Ambient Parking #1" through "Ambient Parking #24." We mixed and rereleased these tracks as streaming audio B-sides over the Internet. Popular response and informal critical attention inspired us to add ever more elaborate explanatory text to our web site. A select bibliography of our sources included:

1) The 2000 post-Kyoto Accord report on automotive fuel emissions in major metropolitan concentrations west of the Rockies.

2) The 1999 Small Business Administration report on wage inequities across gender lines in the private sector.

3) The 1980s Kern County stats on rising rates of bullying among girls, ages eight through thirteen, in the Fresno public school district.

4) The pedagogical philosophies of Count Tolstoy.

5) Marcel Proust's unwritten letters to Alfred Agostinelli, volumes 1 through 3.

6) Several lesser-known Taoist texts.

7) The *Portable New Millennium Anthology of Anti-Late-Consumer-Capitalist Writings*, published by Barnes & Noble.

8) The seminal Technicolor love duets of Rock Hudson and Doris Day.

9) Essays on the unseen footage clipped out by the signature jump cuts of early New Wave cinema, contributing to the development of a hidden hipster mise-en-scène that revealed its holiness, leisurely and progressively, to countless generations of twenty-five year olds.*

In the midst of our compilation, we slipped underground and regrouped to discuss proper ambition. After several cycles of soul-searching, we deemed ourselves ready to produce a full-length album. We purchased sturdy walking shoes and took only public transit in order to develop rigorous objectivity vis-à-vis our subject matter. A period of intensive study ensued.

We positioned ourselves near the entrances of major garage structures in the core of the city to observe the tonal differences between midweek and weekend parking. We rode the elevators to roof level, where prime parking spots and a crosshatched walkway led to scenic aerial dining. We patrolled the grounds of self-attended corner lots, where visitors parked between divisions of cracked asphalt and inserted dollar bills into numbered slots on metal collection boxes.

We compared the tempos of residential versus commercial parking, noting the modal distinction between those who parked within twenty feet of their destination and those who parked to walk toward a designated area, such as a faux downtown or pedestrian marketplace. These two populations, as it turned out, were separated culturally and socioeconomically by a chromatic half step. The seductive dissonance of songs-at-war, it seemed, had not been lost on certain city architects.

---

* These sources marked an artist's, or an outlaw's, paradise. And though we saw our own work as emotionally proportionate to them, their appearance here was more realpolitik than academic. We hoped to generate a bibliography so tedious and overgrown that it would be mistaken as our primary preoccupation and prevent scholars from stealing our work. We hoped to create a field of footnotes so perplexing and baroque that critics would feel compelled to write their own criticism of them.

We quit our day jobs and took turns riding shotgun with the meter maids in their electric patrol carts. By sundown, we could distinguish at a glance between red zone, loading zone, time-out, peak-hour, street sweeping, and hillside curbing violations. We issued twenty-five citations in the name of "The Project," each one hand-numbered and signed. Ticket proceeds were wired promptly to our Canoga Park bank account to be tapped for food, outfits for gender reassignment, bail, and the like.

Refreshed and funded, we sprawled into the suburbs and exurbs, commuting by rideshare. In the predawn hours, some of us in orange visibility vests could be seen unlatching the chain ropes that prohibited the public from parking in restricted lots. Others among us staged political experiments involving radical restriping of the yellow and white lines dividing vehicle spaces. One morning in the faculty-reserved lot of a local elementary school, all lines formed closed rectangles, rendering legal entry into the spaces impossible. A state of emergency was declared and all educational activities were halted for the better part of a week.

We reconnoitered the perimeter of an outlet mall and tested the sound characteristics of each parking zone, as denoted by color and letter. "Red G" had the best acoustics, while "Yellow M" enchanted several of us with its pastoral wind-organ effects. A rich tradition of sound emerged from this most unmusical of landscapes. The bus shelter was our banjo solo, the Wide and Tall store our barbershop quartet, the big-box superstore our stadium rock band. Wandering through an overflow parking lot, we could almost hear the invisible, hysterical crowd screaming for more, calling out the names of coveted brands of merchandise.

But we were not dawdling here to produce another humdinger New Age epic. We boxed up our demo tapes and hiked to the nearest all-you-can-eat buffet. Commanding office hours there for the better part of the day, we plotted the emergence of a new cadence of parking—not just the parking lot but the hum of engines in idle, not just the cars in action but the action without the cars, the pure gestalt of parking itself.

Presenting our latest efforts to the public, we set up shop in a large recreational park bordering a well-heeled neighborhood and played for tips. Our contributions to civic life went largely unappreciated. We examined our collection jar. On the first day, we earned a handful of Styrofoam peanuts, a brass button, forty-four cents in grimy change, two expired bus tickets, a mangled dog collar, and a plumber's snake.

On the second day, we earned several pieces of lint from a lime-green polyester garment, a Canadian nickel, a torn-off fragment from the Book of Ecclesiastes, a crumpled love note on wide-ruled paper, a bus schedule, and an infant's pacifier. On the sixth day, we exchanged high-fives with the elderly woman who tended the tamale cart near the park entrance. On the eleventh day, we received our first outburst of spontaneous applause, from a gawky adolescent clutching a dog-eared edition of *Being and Time*.

The next day was Saturday. For two sets of forty minutes each, we enjoyed a modest audience of weekenders who listened with perplexed curiosity and clapped politely. Families collected on the grass. Newborns strapped in baby carriers gazed at us in stupefied fascination. The crowd thinned as the lunch hour approached. A fresh audience gathered by midafternoon, but we were soon upstaged by a skilled kazoo player performing the highlights from a recent Three Tenors concert.

Days thirteen and fourteen were largely uneventful.

As dusk fell on the fifteenth day, a pack of coyotes could be heard in the distance, responding to our set with piteous, drawn-out howls. We stopped playing at once, hearkening to the sounds of primordial woe. At first we saw ourselves as allies with this invisible faction of the animal kingdom. Our powers of cross-species communication impressed us to no end. Yet when we packed up for the evening and headed for the lights of a pedestrian exit, we imagined the canines lying in wait for us with bristling fur and bared teeth, ready to lunge at our naked throats. Hustling up the sidewalk with armloads of equipment, we attracted bewildered looks from passing drivers. After fifteen minutes of discombobulated running, our panic finally subsided. We found ourselves standing in a mini-mall amidst a crowd of blasé evening shoppers, mere blocks away from the park.

The next day, we resumed our rustic residency with a sense of foreboding. We played softly and tentatively under the watchful eyes of hawks and ravens, careful not to upset the hidden wildlife. When park visitors stopped to drop change in our tip jar and compliment us on our perseverance, they were startled when we shushed them and pointed anxiously toward the hills.

As days passed, we endured foxtails, stinging nettles, poison oak, and other instances of botanical aggression. Swarms of mosquitoes learned of our whereabouts and made special detours to feast on us. Even the koi seemed unusually belligerent, hurling their bodies high in the air and slapping down hard against the water, as we crept past the lily pond. Reduced to swollen and itchy specimens of paranoia, we clung to our instruments in desperation, summoning up overtones of combustion engines and squealing tires to ward off our fear.

On the twenty-first day, we had unseasonably hot weather. Seeking a cooler post, we stationed ourselves near the edge of the pond. Within moments, a gaggle of geese waddled toward us with meaning and purpose. We pushed on with our set, striving to ignore the scores of beady eyes fixed upon us. Like their human counterparts, the birds had struck a devil's bargain, migrating along a network of artificial ponds that enabled their survival but trapped them in a pattern of dependence. As we accelerated toward the climax of another ambient pileup, a collective honking and hissing erupted, and the geese rushed us. Our attempts at self-defense were feeble and inadequate. Snatching our equipment from flapping wings and snapping bills, we fled to the park exit. For weeks afterward, we were traumatized by nightly images of the avian confrontation.

Clearly, we were not cut out for the vicissitudes of exurban living. Ignored by the gentry and rejected by the flora and fauna, we resolved to limit our explorations to the metropolis. Slathering ourselves anew with zinc oxide and mosquito repellent, we bushwhacked to a busy roadway and gazed longingly at the vehicles with passengers riding inside, protectively enclosed in speeding carapaces of metal and glass.

Once we reached the city, we sought safety in numbers and traveled with a clique of self-taught urbanists. Lured by their bohemian-intellectual fashion sense which seemed to boost our own attractiveness by mere proximity, we followed them deep into the heart of the motorized landscape. Revved-up engines tugged at our heartstrings. Featureless roadways called out to us. Particles of dust and smog rained down on us. How could we explain the boundless joy we felt, which was also a boundless dread?

Like synthetic geologists, we marveled at the diverse materials in our environment: tempered glass, pneumatic rubbers, plastics in pastel colors, floor mats designed to cushion the feet of weary shoppers and boisterous schoolchildren, concrete barriers ingeniously contoured to guide swerving vehicles away from one another.

We walked for miles alongside a retaining wall, admiring its colored tiles depicting the sun, moon, and stars in modern-day hieroglyphics. When we reached the end, we came upon an underground parking garage famed for its advances in lighting and spent a good hour there studying the lamps lining its vaults. A laminated placard posted nearby aided us in our efforts:

> Welcome. These lamps were designed to simulate torches mounted on the walls of caverns in Neolithic times. The tungsten bulbs emit a tight range of frequencies at the red-orange end of the spectrum, thought to evoke the awe and wonder experienced by the primitive psyche in the presence of fire. In studies, these lights were proven to help conduct traffic in a descending spiral and calm the aggressions of frustrated drivers. Their most interesting feature, however, is the versatile substance that makes up their casings. Invented by an army scientist in 1942, this compound was promptly heralded as the wonder metal of the future. In cold temperatures, it serves as an excellent conductor of electricity. And when stretched into a thin sheet and struck by a practiced hand, it resounds with the pure tones of the pentatonic scale. Since 1997, industrial designers have repurposed it as a stain-resistant material for use in lightweight medical applications. Luminous, ductile, and impervious to moisture, this splendid alloy is already being utilized by vanguard orthodontists to straighten preadolescent teeth.

Under the guidance of our new companions, we learned to celebrate abject sites and degraded regions of geography. We haunted neighborhoods of foreclosed real estate. We wandered reverently through a homeless encampment of corrugated sheet-metal dwellings and pit fires. Our romantic dystopian side was nurtured by visions of early evening light glancing off the conveyor bridges of a defunct vegetable cannery. A silkscreened sign for canned peas inspired us to freeze in our tracks and wax poetic. We shopped for groceries at a government surplus store, jostling for aisle space with new immigrants and the working poor.

We felt exalted by the edifying scenes of blight but soon found ourselves shrinking from the accompanying minilectures, which the urbanists inserted at every tableau and pit stop like a didactic soundtrack. It became impossible to stroll down the street leisurely without one of them bemoaning the onslaught of neighborhood gentrification or global capitalism, as evidenced by a boarded-up storefront or new condominium complex.

Tensions mounted as our antipathy toward the urbanists grew. We winced at their omniscient posturing and finger pointing. We cringed at their critical theory, which they disseminated with all the single-minded fervor of a fundamentalist campaign. One day, as they tucked into a diatribe against the sterile interchangeability of fast-food franchises, we realized that a serious injustice was taking place. Seizing them by the shoulders, we pushed them inside our favorite restaurant and into our favorite plastic dining booth. Shocked by the experience of being touched or even worse manhandled, they took in our raised voices with blank faces: "There is no other burger joint in the world quite like our burger joint. This is our burger joint filled with our unique burger joint memories, and you will never take it away from us!"

A parting of ways with the urbanists soon followed. After an initial wave of self-doubt and insecurity, we came to bask in the renewed autonomy of our position. Released from the chains of our intellect, we indulged the full fancies of our id, and our unfettered noodling soon resulted in a string of underground ambient hits.

We became one with the bus garages, auto dealer lots, and slick consumer parkades. Our lyric force billowed out like a canopy over vast fairgrounds of snoozing hoods and fenders.

We got intimately acquainted with city street corners, where people met up before striking out for drinks. Our recordings streamed into sidewalk grates and tunneled through sewage pipes, percolating nightly from steam vents like great belches of the civilized world. Sleek Mercedes coupes owed their unexpected rumblings to our compositional experiments. Musclebound Mustangs sampled our tracks as they surged through the streets with the power of two hundred flatulent horses.

One day after wandering the city, we came to rest on a public bench opposite a cloverleaf offramp. We watched a steady stream of cars emerge from the freeway, engines still hot from overdrive, windshields ablaze with magnified reflections of sunlight. We became transfixed by the facial expressions of the drivers, some stoic and resigned, others contorted and cranky, still others caught in moments of deep personal compromise as they wiped away tears, fingered a nostril, or belted out the vocals to a popular yet embarrassing song on the radio. Only the automobile could offer such a transparent shell, such a convincing yet ineffective theater of privacy.

Fascinated, we longed to join this motorized society. After debating the idea for days as we applied moleskin to blisters on our feet, we broke down and bought a used car.

As the ignition spark fired and the engine roared into life, all our troubles seemed to melt away. Automated travel eased us into an anesthetized state. We no longer fussed over trivial concerns or worried about the government. Our usual aches and pains vanished to be replaced with leg cramps from the labor of constant acceleration. Yet we happily endured this minor discomfort for the sake of the petrol-propelled cause. The tempo of human experience was quickening, and we were not about to be left behind on the pavement.

When we attempted eye contact with other drivers, most threw us reproachful looks and rolled up their windows, visibly irked. Undeterred, we set out in pursuit of the ideal mobile community. We greeted crossing guards with esoteric hand signals and cozied up to highway patrol. We commiserated with commuters and flirted with motorcycle gangs. Eventually, a transient population took notice. A busload of tourists pointed at our car and snapped photos. A patient reclining on an ambulance stretcher waved weakly to us through the red-flashing rear window. Small children presiding over the backseats of station wagons pulled rubber faces at us.

Like born-again motorists, we savored the blur of shapes and colors streaming past our windows. Scenery that had never made much sense to us on the ground assumed a spectacular logic at sixty-five-plus miles per hour. Overhead signs formed sentences. Electronic alert boards broadcasting urgent public messages punctuated the horizon. The world was full of texts meant for zooming giants, and we pitied the poor souls who were condemned to navigate this baffling vastness on foot. The walkers were illiterate but content, stumbling past fragments of meaning without care or comprehension. We, on the other hand, were speed-readers of the landscape, subject to the simultaneous rapture and burden of our gift.

We lived a large-scale existence, rapidly skimming the saga of the coastline, the memoir of the beach, the testimony of the sand. Whole towns and bedroom communities flickered past us like skipped pages. Clumps of drought-tolerant vegetation decorated the margins. The moral of this roadside fable shone forth in ticking mile markers, indicating just how far we had traveled in the blink of an eye.

We zoomed toward the outlands, where drooping electrical wires traced patterns of drift and escape. We hurtled into the hinterlands, where underground silos housed long-range ballistic missiles.

Smog was a steady artifact, a low-lying smear across a canvas of middling air. Against this backdrop of synthetic particles, the oleander shrubs with their pink and white flowers served as enduring reminders of our origins. In the early morning hours, an abstract community of birds and bees stirred into action, transforming the landscape into a nocturnal tropic of song. By dawn, nothing would remain of this concert but the yellow dust of pollination and a few dropped feathers.

Sadly, our reveries were shattered by the greatest nuisance of the road: other drivers. Like a new strain of virus multiplying at greater and greater rates, they filed onto the freeway, blocking our progress and monopolizing the diamond lane. Where at one time we might have longed for their company, we now simply wished they would disappear. We rolled down our windows and shouted insults into the air. We made obscene gestures. We swerved from lane to lane, initiating tailgating contests. We sat through endless miles of gridlock, cursing the onset of overpopulation that had spoiled our exclusive romance with the road.

When a blanket of pollution descended upon the land, our road rage gave way to bouts of asthma. We coughed, and the greater metropolitan region coughed with us. Gasping, we struggled to fill our lungs as neon clouds drifted unheeded across the horizon. When our symptoms subsided, a host of allergies set in. Wadded-up facial tissue collected in our car door pockets. Convulsive sneezing disrupted our steering. The exhaust trailed us in a haze, seeping into our pores and threatening to transform our cells into malignant shapes and sizes.

On our days off-road, we threw ourselves anew into our work, but success continued to elude us. Our appeals to the music establishment were rejected, our requests for gigs ridiculed and denied. When we offered to open for a mildly famous singer-songwriter, his backup band coolly looked us over head to toe and exhaled smoke in our faces. We resorted to crashing open-mike sessions only to be escorted to the sidewalk by humorless bouncers. Out of necessity, we returned to our usual haunts of open-air lots and nocturnal garages, performing for a scant audience of ne'er-do-wells and fellow ambient artists.

At long last, our vinyl single was picked up by a DJ at a local college radio station. Scouring the print media for reviews, we found our record mentioned in a parenthetical statement at the end of the pop-culture column of an obscure submetropolitan weekly. With bated breath and pounding hearts, we read the review:

> (As for "Ambient Parking #25," this mindless, if hellishly beautiful, composition cannot possibly have sprung from any relevant artists, whether aesthetic, social, or political. Its half-baked origin undermines musicians who deem it proper to start from somewhere real, and its repository of amplified drone signifies an ideology of deep and troubling indifference. It's beyond selling out. It's the kind of work that celebrates playgrounds for cars and driving for pleasure. Musically and environmentally, it's an abomination. To the recording artists, we plead: spare us your

"talents." Channel your enthusiasm into less tedious outlets, and leave the dismantling of the superstructures to our beloved and much decorated philosophers.)

Vexed by the critique yet grateful for the publicity, we repaired to our flat and awaited signs of reactive fallout. Before too long, a backlash movement gathered momentum. Radio listeners dialed the station in force, requesting play of our single for birthdays, pajama parties, and late-night lovers' apologies. Foes of the columnist exhorted their friends and colleagues to buy our record, launching it well into the top 500s on the indie charts. A countercriticism was authored, its words disseminated in the form of street fliers, bathroom graffiti, and other lo-fi memes. One young lady was moved to write a letter to the editor of the weekly:

Dear Editor,

Although I graduated from college a few years ago, I still have my radio tuned to KVRM, my source for new music. For those who don't know, KVRM plays releases from the Ambient Parkers every third Tuesday of the month from eleven to midnight.

I'm writing to protest your columnist's review of "Ambient Parking #25." Since discovering this band, I've downloaded all their tracks and burned dozens of CDs for my friends. Last year, I even stumbled upon the Ambient Parkers in the middle of a recording session. I'm pretty sure the double honk at the end of "Ambient Parking #9" is me on my Vespa. (I had to honk to stop a minivan from backing into me.)

I'm totally devoted to this band for reasons your columnist just wouldn't understand. After graduating with honors in English, I took my essays on Blake and Derrida as writing samples to Career Day. When I got there, I found out that the entire auditorium was reserved for science and engineering majors. Two tables were set up outside for recruiters of liberal arts students: one for a coffee chain hiring baristas and another for an office complex hiring receptionists and stock boys. Determined to become a journalist, I mailed my résumé to all the local newspapers. Six months later, I had sampled every flavor of ice cream in the freezer aisle, while my follow-up letters to editors like yourself remained unanswered.

How can I explain what the Ambient Parkers and their music have done for me? I now work at the Caffeine Nation in the mall, which has a multilevel garage for parking. After-hours, I meet up with a group of my friends and we wander through the garage, dancing and laughing deliriously among the rows of cars. Cars back up and car alarms go off in the distance, just like the finale of "Ambient Parking #25." With the music humming in my ears, I feel slightly lost but with company.

Heather

Captivated, we revisited the letter endlessly, pausing to pore over its more flattering passages. We felt vindicated and confirmed, our labors recognized at last. For several days, we promenaded the avenues with our heads held high and our chests puffed out. One motorist slowed down to salute us, tossing waxed fruit and other tributes in our direction. A barefoot entourage latched onto us, strewing our path with confetti. No one could challenge our victimized superiority. When two police officers accosted us, we fell to the ground groveling until they threw up their hands and backed away, mortified.

Spurred by Heather's declarations, we rounded up all the copies of our negative reviews and set them aflame. We envisioned the resulting bonfire blazing for seven days and seven nights, scorching the cement yard and illuminating the sky over a ten-block radius. In reality, the papers curled in the flames for twenty minutes before crumpling in a charred heap. Festivities soon unfolded around the smoke. Friends and acquaintances arrived, loaded with party platters and cases of beer. Finger foods passed from hand to mouth and refreshments flowed freely from pitchers. As the evening progressed, singing contests broke out, spanning everything from mid-Atlantic sea shanties to Central Asian throat chanting. Drunken orators vied for top honors, and the city block resounded with the thunder of our carousing.

We awoke the next morning sprawled beneath a layer of ash and debris. A shambling silence had spread throughout the flat, displacing the barbaric yawps and whoops of the previous night. Anxious to get busy with new work, we cast open the blinds, shooed away our groupies, and mixed up a set of hangover cocktails.

Strapping on our equipment, we immersed ourselves in an ambitious recording session that spanned the downtown fashion district. A stringent policy was adopted with respect to distractions. Conversations were stifled and our nutrients were limited to leftovers handed to us by well-dressed couples walking past. In the midst of a four-track sound collage, a handsome orange tabby approached us, but we resisted the urge to pet it more than once. Satisfied at last with the extent of our material, we staggered home, dropped our packs on the floor, and passed out cold.

We turned to the raw tapes the next day, only to recoil in dismay. Out of fourteen-plus hours of audio, only twenty minutes were deemed usable. The remainder was a noisy mess dominated by sentimental clichés and lyric conformity. Overwrought feedback loops told the tale of our neurotic intervention. After attempts at consoling one another, we tried to articulate the root of our failure. "Our tweaking of the special effects could use some serious fine-tuning," one of us remarked. "We should have refrained from anthropomorphizing the parking lot and allowed it to express its natural state," ventured another. "Egoism has no place in endeavors of this scope and magnitude," we concurred. We jotted down our assessments on scraps of paper and dropped them into the cardboard suggestion box, which served as a storehouse for our inspirational ideas.*

Ever resourceful, we salvaged what we could to assemble "Ambient Parking #26." A nervous pressure filled the studio as we assessed long measures and varying time signatures, the buzz that underpinned our sense of urgency. Released on a DIY label together with two bonus B-sides, the extended-play single was quickly snapped up by our fans and became a surprise hit among midnight trainspotters.

As with previous releases, the music continued to lure us. There was more new ground waiting to be discovered, more parking lots left unsung. We were impatient to reach the next asphalt frontier, the next prairie of stalls. Public squares were fords to be crossed; automated tollbooths and horizontal swing-armed gates were obstacles to be surmounted. Like pioneers, we were eager to sink our stakes into plots of unclaimed land, where automobiles proliferated in quiescent herds.

One morning, we trailed a stampede of traffic to a manicured office park. After examining the hedges for acoustics and dampening effects, we sat on a curb and watched office workers stream in through the revolving front doors. Executive jingles ushered us into an era of patriotic optimism. Broadband network

---

* This unassuming archive had rescued us from many bleak hours and dead-end jam sessions. The mere fact of its existence reassured us during moments of insecurity. Often, we were able to jump-start our creative flow simply by reaching into the box and fluttering its pages in contemplation.

transmissions relayed messages of financial confidence. With this much synergy and venture capital in the air, how could anything possibly go wrong?

Boarding the company shuttle as pro bono entertainers, we serenaded the working elite with motivational tunes. After a run-in with a security guard, we alighted from the shuttle, tucked in our shirttails, and clutched marketing brochures in an effort to blend in. Strolling along shrub-lined walkways, we conversed in pleasant tones and peppered our speech with business jargon. We toured the emerging markets, plucking low-hanging fruit from the trees of opportunity. The developing world rebounded after a series of major climatic disasters, while a construction boom in Eastern Europe sweetened the returns on our aggressively indexed portfolio. But when the profit margins of our vanity dot-com start-up achieved less than impactful results at quarter's end, we liquidated our holdings and took up the twelve-bar blues.

Our view was occasionally spoiled by the spectacle of other people. Visitors loitered near the lobby entrance, gossiping loudly and throwing our subwoofer levels out of whack. Joggers spun out from the revolving doors with bright eyes, running past their heavyset coworkers. When a pair of cardio-walkers came close to clipping our heels, we swiftly diverted our course and sought refuge near a large garbage bin. Cloaked by the odor of rotting waste, we crouched in silence until the fitness enthusiasts passed safely out of sight.

At day's end, we trekked along the perimeter of the office park and came upon a pavilion nestled in a sleepy lagoon. Climbing roses formed an archway around its pillars and royal carpets of moss graced its steps. We sat on a stone bench at its center, where we watched ducks float by in clucking pairs and soft breezes stir gentle waves in the water. Although we admired the pavilion and its water garden, we checked our watches and hurried onward. We were lured once again by the seven-story parking garage, whose steel girders and billowing fumes could be glimpsed just ahead.

After succumbing to the workday grind, we found ourselves with pockets of cash ready to be dished out to the entertainment sector. We dispatched our most gifted members to the theater district to pose as valet parking escorts. Unfortunately, none of them qualified for the job. Still all were able to observe, with noses incautiously close to the chain-link fence, how the intervals of time between drop-offs and pickups could be exploited as a natural rhythm. After closing hour, improvisations of this rhythm in the dark formed the basis of a musical breakthrough, later unveiled in a single entitled "Ambient Parking for the Rich and Famous."

Then the economy collapsed and our theory was discarded in favor of an aesthetic of banal scarcity. Secular pragmatism replaced the faith-based work ethic, which had once led to the lush arpeggios of grocery bags being loaded into single-driver vehicles and trunk lids thumping to a close in the late afternoon sunlight. Energy costs soared and we began to ration usage of our recording equipment. When blackouts rolled through the region, we huddled in the hydrangea bushes and meditated on the functional relationship between white stripes and klieg lighting.

One day without warning, terrorists attacked several government buildings, including the county DMV. We rushed onto the scene with fluorescent cones, converting the DMV garage into a triage center. The injuries we witnessed there illustrated just how easily the luxury zone of the parking lot could be extended to slaughter. Over the next eighteen months, we were flooded with media images showing the impact of retaliatory airstrikes and a coordinated ground campaign on so-called enemy soil.

In the lot of an abandoned manufacturing plant, we commissioned a troupe of our dancer friends to stage Butoh-inflected body movements simulating the trauma of the violence. With eyes drooped down and mouths twisted into ghastly shapes, the dancers mimicked the expressions of citizens trapped in the rubble of urban warfare. Meanwhile, we played the role of embedded journalists, inserting audiotapes of convoy trucks in the process of backing up, parking, unloading supplies, and being otherwise absorbed in the business of large-scale First World logistics. We procured a white utility van from a police auction and programmed it to circumscribe and videotape the performances at a rate of 1.26 miles per hour.

While some dancers engaged in the primacy of the open wound, others explored the reactions of the general public, manifesting looks of shock and horror as they mimed long sessions of compulsive news watching. Still others dramatized the disintegration of human flesh into powdery dust, falling to the ground as one and draping themselves with a colossal black sheet. Like lovers and enablers, we mopped up their sweat and tended to their agonies. When their suffering threatened to plateau, we pushed forth convincing stage props representing shrapnel and fire to enhance the verisimilitude of their contortions.

One dancer's performance in particular gave rise to intolerable feelings. A hushed audience generated by word of mouth began to gather respectfully. Enacting the plight of a disaster victim, she placed herself inside the wreckage of a crushed vehicle. With her arms wedged against her chest and her legs pinned together, she conjured up a pathos of immobility.

The dancer's choreography was subtle and wrenching in nature. She began by executing a series of muscular convulsions, emanating from the pit of her stomach and rippling upward, to dislodge a cell phone from her breast pocket. By rocking her elbows left and right, she nudged the instrument millimeter by millimeter along the length of her forearms, until it arrived at her hands. For a quarter of an hour, her fingers simply wriggled in the air, prompting a few of us to swoon from suspense. At last her fingertips touched down on the keypad. She attempted the three-digit emergency plea followed by the speed-dialing of loved ones, yet her appeals were rebuffed every time. A courteous prerecorded voice explained that, due to heavy network traffic, her call could not be completed at this time.*

Distressed by the performance, we prayed for its swift end, but to no avail. The dancer was committed to the integrity of her suffering, and we in turn were bound to the extremity of her commitment. Over the next ten hours, her fingers gradually moved across the keypad to invoke ever more elaborate and futile combinations of numbers. Her solitude was consummate and philosophic, that of a lone survivor in a parking lot marked for death. As she punched in the numbers, the space between her fingers, the phone, and the wreckage was filled in with *ambience*, a covert backdrop of collective amnesia and white noise impeding her efforts to secure voice contact with a savior. Thus did her motions of survival approach the sublime abstraction of art. Converted, we stood by in admiration, safeguarding her self-expression and shooing away the philistines who threatened to revive her with the Jaws of Life.

---

* Although we had prepared an ambient soundtrack to complement the dancer's performance, we chose not to play it, relying purely on sounds generated by the dancer and her cell phone. We hoped the effect would challenge our assumptions about the range of audibility associated with stillness, that is, the conventional parked position.

To our amazement, the number of spectators only grew over time. They squatted in tight clusters with blankets and warm refreshment, digging in for their wordless vigil. By the eleventh hour, battery levels in the dancer's phone dropped to critical, dimming the LCD and plunging our stage view into darkness. Sound lingered on as our sole medium of recognition. The pressing of alphanumeric keys continued to reach our hearing, though in fainter tones and at reduced tempo. Sighs and groans sang forth at intervals from the dancer, interspersed with spasms of belabored breathing. We entered a stage of exalted anticipation, as we awaited the apotheosis of the performance.

Suddenly all sound inside the wreckage puckered into a pause and then, just as quietly, ceased. The staged death of the dancer gradually registered with the audience, but our astonishment at what we had originally conceived as a larger-than-life experience was soon replaced with emptiness. The subsequent dismantling of the set was similarly anticlimactic, yet worthy of note. Some of us waited and wept in solemn queues to give the dancer hugs as she emerged from her post, hungry and shivering and too weary for words. Others lunged forward to attack the wreckage in a spasm of fury. A few of us, however, turned away and shuddered with our eyes cast dreadfully to the ground, because we had witnessed—in the cosmic space of time between the onslaught of disaster and the reinstatement of the parking lot—the living performer become a thing.[*]

---

[*] In retrospect, it would have been far better to have used a puppet rather than a live performer on the stage, as in those serial dramas and films derived from a uniquely Asiatic sensibility, in which introspection requires a collective look backward into generations enclosed by regret and longing (through the use of flashbacks and hesitant dialogue inching bit by bit behind a mask of shame), and in which a wooden acting style is used to embody the depersonalized moment (or the moment of noisy stillness), where the effects of trauma have finally spread in closeup over the entire face and the resulting countenance, devoid of all Western forms of expression, is assumed by a figure who, having survived one too many atrocities along with a historical experience so annihilating as to arouse the sympathy of future spectators, is forced to step back and cover his face.

The performance haunted us for several weeks and then depressed us for many more. On the street, proponents of agitprop celebrated our collaborative efforts by distributing leaflets in our honor. Precocious art students were spotted wearing T-shirts commemorating the event. Eschewing the fanfare, our dancer friends packed up and retreated to a co-op in the composers' quarter of former East Berlin. Six weeks later, they resurfaced on the front lawn of our nation's capital, where they had choreographed a massive sit-in against the war. From a semisecure wireless location on the southwest corner of the lawn, they called our flat, but none of us felt remotely well enough to answer the phone.

We languished in curious isolation for some time, venturing out only to gather newspapers and pilfer milk. With backs aching from prolonged political engagement, we lay on our sides, reaching up from time to time to accept offerings of medicinal tea. The din of car alarms on the street exacerbated our mental imbalance. We began wandering outside at night in a sleepless daze, our eyes bleary and bloodshot, our ears stuffed with cotton to block out the now painful effects of ambient noise. Muttering dully to ourselves, we clambered over barriers to follow the winding routes of trolley tracks and other dormant passages. Service tunnels drew us deeper into the melancholia of forsaken industrial sites. Over the freight yards and scrap yards we went, seeking warmth from the fires of hobo encampments. Dawn found us slumped against the mosaic tiles of a remote subway entrance, blinking wearily as we waited for the gates to open and another long day to begin.

We lost faith in the radical ideals of experimental art. Highbrow culture repulsed us, even as upper middlebrow culture drew us like moths to a flame. In our quest for timeless truisms in the face of mortal suffering, we developed an unhealthy attachment to confessional poetry. Numerous manifestations of the genre—

some with tattered first-edition covers, others with glossy book jackets exhibiting meteoric praise and brooding photographs of the authors—began to amass on our bedside tables. We read late into the night, hanging upon every word, comparing each poet's lofty predicament to our own.

It was only a matter of time before our literary habit blossomed into a full-blown addiction. Midway through breakfast, our eyes opened wide as we were gripped by a vague panic. We dropped our spoons and rushed off to compose a slim volume of metrical couplets dedicated to the poignant futility of the human condition. Reciting the lines to one another, we held our chins pensively and nodded our heads knowingly. Aware that the sublime was often cloaked in the mundane, we soon found it impossible to shop for organic pluots or feed our past-bloom orchids without experiencing paroxysms of feeling. The cawing of a crow in a placid suburban lane recalled memories from an unhappy childhood, along with the many misdeeds committed in thoughtless innocence. Speechless with shame, we vowed to prostrate ourselves before that fierce and fickle mistress, Redemption.

When we failed to attain forgiveness, a drastic nihilism spread through our ranks. We awoke each morning and locked ourselves in the bathroom, where we grimaced into the mirror and studied our distorted countenances. The world was bleak and gray and devoid of meaning. The banality of our daily affairs was broken only by the chaos of our mood swings, as we oscillated between maudlin sympathy for all sentient beings and snarling contempt for our fellow man. Sullen and peevish, we loitered near a promenade and talked among ourselves, calling attention to the personal shortcomings of passersby and their children. The fun of inventing these insults lifted our spirits and we were surprised to feel lightness in our being, as if our nastiness was fulfilling a deep therapeutic need. But before too long, an angry mob closed in on us. Looking up at the sky, we silently prayed for deliverance until they finished their denouncement and withdrew.

Our truculence soon gave way to immovable lethargy. For days, we slumbered until noon, retiring to the couch for a quality nap at three-thirty. Our few lucid hours were filled with the artistry of attentive apathy. We found ourselves in limbo, vacillating between day and night, and tried to kill time by humming the theme from "Ambient Parking #3" at a deadly mezzo piano. We continued unabated through the night until half past ten the next morning, when a quorum of us detached abruptly from the sound loop. Four members moved out that very day and gave up ambient recording altogether. Of these four, two founded an emo-pop band in the bowels of Los Angeles, one ran for public office, and one embarked on an abortive writing career, penning ninety-six forgettable sonnets before enrolling in graduate studies on the persistence of obscurity.

The sudden defections depleted our spirits. In our depression, we took to subsisting on handfuls of dry cereal and drips from a leaky kitchen faucet. We stared out the window with our knees drawn up, twirling our forelocks. Although we apprehended decay, we were powerless to arrest it. In the meantime, we fell victim to a host of afflictions, a short list of which included: fatigue, moodiness, dizziness, migraine, insomnia, narcolepsy, sleep apnea, charley horse, halitosis, toothache, indigestion, lactose intolerance, anemia, eczema, hives, sneezing, sniffling, congestion, hacking cough, chills, and the grippe. Dogs barked at us on the street, aghast at our sickly, shriveled appearance. Fresh-faced children on their way home from school took turns humiliating us with rhymes. Just when it seemed we could sink no lower, mice raided our flat one night, pillaging our stores of corn flakes, flaky toast, and toasted wheat.

At last dawn arrived and a slender shaft of light gleamed upon our darkest hour. A self-controlled efficiency lumbered into our consciousness, if only to mask our malaise. New projects arose on the horizon, as we extracted inspiration from the twentieth-century coterie of artists formerly known as the avant-garde. We performed Iyengar's standing tree pose each morning, while attuning our ears to the microsymphonies of flawed indoor plumbing. We held symposiums on the merits of warm water baths. We hid behind fortresses of books, training our minds and steeling our bodies for attack. We composed an alternative instrumental score for the *Bhagavad Gita* and played it for each other on washboard and spoons.

A regimen of devout asceticism strengthened our resolve. With discriminating eyes, we cleared out our closets, streamlined our larder, and put our more frivolous possessions out on the sidewalk. Our David Carradine memorabilia soon vanished on a kick scooter, while a family of four absconded with our beanbag set. In lieu of proper furniture, we sat back-to-back with one another for orthopedic support, reading serial Victorian novels aloud to while away the nights. On our rare outings into town, we took to draping blankets around our shoulders, less as a fashion statement than as a makeshift solution for keeping warm, having dispensed with our Gore-Tex jackets in a fit of worldly renunciation.

Content in our newfound independence, we tried fermenting our own yogurt and tofu. On a narrow strip of soil along the south wall of our flat, we cultivated eggplant, zucchini, and runner beans, while heirloom tomatoes flourished on the rooftop. Dividing up the harvest, we set aside half as raw produce and incorporated the other half into single-serving meals. We established a barter system with other ambient artists, providing home goods in exchange for prerelease CDs, backstage passes, and state-of-the-art recording equipment.

Our cockeyed optimism was revived by classic Broadway show tunes, which we played one after another on a secondhand turntable. The heavy doors of our hearts creaked open as earnest voices belted out sentiments too private to surface in ordinary conversation, yet welcome as bursts of unnatural song. Momentarily released from the shackles of irony, we inwardly wept to the solos of *Camelot*, *Fiddler on the Roof*, and *Paint Your Wagon*. As we listened to an extended duet, we meditated on the resiliency of a love that refused to stop harmonizing.

We became devoted students of our dreams and sought to fulfill their uncanny expectations in waking life. The appearance of a red trombone in one of our dreams prompted us to debate its significance over breakfast the next morning. We reviewed our listening knowledge of several trombone concertos, hoping to dredge up subconscious origins of insight and meaning. We filled our windows with hundreds of origami trombones, and the spectacle soon drew a neighborhood following, garnering a boxed write-up in the free downtown weekly. While we prowled restlessly upstairs, controversy erupted on the sidewalk and added a few beats to the word on the street: *What madness had seized the Ambient Parkers now? Would they turn acoustic and remix "Ambient Parking #25" with horns? Had they given up pure ambience for the easy listening of Carnegie Hall?*

SOURCEBOOK

Sitting at the kitchen table after another homegrown meal, we pushed our chairs back and reflected. Within moments, we heard a motorcycle revving up outside our flat, sputtering and kicking before barreling off into the distance. Touched by the sounds, we remembered the thunderous assembly of Harleys with gleaming drive trains that we had captured on audio at a small-town hog rally and sampled in "Ambient Parking #5."

We gathered on the hearth rug and swapped stories before a blazing log fire, our toes stretched out toward the flames. As time wore on, our reminiscing brought us out of idle, shifting gears into reverse and rolling backward until we vowed to unmask the soul or essential character of every parking lot in recent memory. We turned once again to our recordings, listening to each session at double, half, then quarter speed, in an effort to disclose sound patterns that might have eluded us in real time.

Through these efforts, we came to recognize the difference between ambient narrative and lyric. Ambient narrative emerged from the daily circuit of residential and commercial lots: slow lanes, stopovers, and pit stops. Ambient lyric was generated through feats of monumental engineering: double-helix parking structures with genetically inspired paths spiraling cars up one way and down another, bombastic freeways with cloverleaf offramps shooting vehicles off in all directions like split atoms.

We surrendered to both forms of ambience and viewed them as distinctive movements of a composition that we listened to compulsively, like tonal junkies. We compiled our findings into a three-part retrospective and uploaded it to our web site as scrolling wallpaper text. Taken together, these fragments immortalized our early career, when we championed authentic experience and plunged headlong into the romance of the overlooked space:

1

We were born in the back of a moving vehicle, coursing past the fields of titanium and clover that marked the settlements of a bold and indolent tomorrow. The beholding of this scene was ephemeral, yet persisted long enough to color the mood and intonations of our first words. We surfaced from slumber, gurgling impressions of truck horns and carburetors, ham signals and telegraph buzz. Ours was the first generation to feel nostalgia for consumer appliances promising artificial repose. When our favorite projection machine was declared obsolete, we wept with a bitterness that enfolded the greater plots and vistas of our childhood.

Art shadowed us with all the fidelity of a nonnegotiable companion. We were raised inside the narratives of residential planners who named treelined streets after poets, boulevards after engineers. Sidewalks surrounded us in flowing streams of silver that paved over our seismic unrest. In the vast determination of this landscape novel, living things were consigned to the backdrop. Retaining walls became our guardians, the overpass our hero. The conflict between eucalyptus and smog would never be rightly resolved.

Yet out of this gridlocked tundra, there emerged a figure who came to occupy the center of our lives. Walking along forbidden thoroughfares lined by walled-off subdivisions until he reached the ocean's edge, he declared himself an enemy of progress.

The official note was resignation, the official tune estrangement, as we mixed and distorted our composition to coax our avatar out of exile. Mentored by his discontent, guided by his sorrow, we became bad subjects, perfectly unfit for day camp, standardized tests, and weekend play dates. We lapsed into a delinquency characterized by the consumption of retail goods and controlled substances. But in the end, the foundations prevailed. The rains of El Niño passed and the warmth of concrete was restored. We relieved our thirst at faucets of treated water, recirculating our sympathies around the civic drain. What new emotion was this and would we recognize ourselves in it?

On a close summer day, the walker returned from wandering a city steeped in broadcast, with nary a trace of commercial pity. Blazing a trail to the garage that housed our sound stations, he paused to clear his ears. He faltered. He leaned against the upturned cone to listen.

2

Like resident convicts, we marked the passing of our school days. We suffered each our private affliction for many years, composing poignant, unsigned missives to the editors of *Truth* and *Absolute Music*. At last we found each other standing at the jukebox of anonymous sympathy, with an open beer in one hand and a volume of Mary Shelley in the other. From the start, it was clear we intended to remake our moral philosophy together. Arm in arm, we walked unformed into the night, parading our youth to the avenues and stars, stepping in time to the bellows and moans of polished city machinery.

We drank freely and sang. We celebrated the portent of our dawning incandescence. We postured and drew an audience. We hid our feelings inside a warehouse of impressive statements. We fashioned thoughts and dissented. We heedlessly deposed the ruling class and then banded together in a confederacy of languishing spirits.

We proceeded with a courage built on a half-embraced acceptance of ourselves. But the more we dared to approach the cause, the more it receded from us. Was this the negative capability we had been waiting all our lives for? Was this an art? If so, our craft would not look like any other craft. It would take no other shape than the sonic phantasm unfurling in our inner ear.

This historical moment lifted us out of disaffection, ushering us into a kinship with all who had lived and died on the grounds where we were now standing, as transients. When we turned, with our jaws sore from habitual, ready-set determination, we discovered a face staring out at us from the mirror. Fierce, brooding, and fearful, it shifted with concern at the flaws and triumphs reflected in the glassy surface.

Unknowing, we hesitated to make our creature's acquaintance. Oftentimes we doubted. Oftentimes we didn't trust ourselves with the act of trusting. Our pursuits might lead to failure or enact lasting damage on our softer sensibilities, but we were prepared to take these risks. We were ready to stake the next era of our lives on our project's potential, to unearth the sound that would come to haunt us that day and forever.

3

In the months leading up to our debut recording, we clamored at the shores of possibility. Spurred by the challenge of transforming ourselves into worthy agents of our art, we set out to discover our conditions of creation. The conception of our art came to us on a forgettable weekday morning, as we awoke to the ebb and flow of traffic. It took shape on our daily bus route, as the doors wrenched open and deposited us in a vast sea of churning tires.

As our aesthetic matured, we loosened its chords and held it up against the going standard. Not to be satisfied with proven success, we took turns assuming the role of the hardnosed reviewer, who belittled us with bon mots and kept our self-congratulations at bay. Scrutinizing us with an unblinking resistance, our critic coolly evaluated, flicking judgments to the air with every drag of his cigarette. Indulging in a touch of cruelty, he sliced at our flanks to show that we were alive—alive and thrashing, but also flawed, callow, vain, untruthful, and guilty of insufficient depth.

And just then, in the midst of our serial adolescent wounding, permanent change seemed possible. In the structures that surrounded us, did we not perceive a desire for overhaul that was defiant and embittered, or cunning and calculated, or perhaps tender as a hand placed on the warm cheek of another, day after day, in a room flooded with sunlight?

Born parenthetical subjects of a myopic regime, we strived to represent an unspoken sensibility, a nascent and covert counterculture—not the part of the culture that catered to us, but the part that ached, hungry for the dismantling of the complacencies that made daily life bearable but false. But first we had to relinquish the fantasies of the tragic solo artist and rock-'n'-roll suicide. We had to resist the urge to equate ironic lyrics with political protest and nihilistic ballads with revolution.

Our banner went unheeded until the advent of the equinox, when the city had collected its fill of strangers and strivers, summoners and wasted youth. Never before had we felt so available to one another. Our softness was unguarded and our unguardedness was revealed as a sign of power. Mirages called to us from afar, pools of kindness to be lapped up by our eager, puppyish humanity. We turned to the world. Roaming the outskirts of the half-excavated city, we stumbled onto a concrete lot. We marked the experience "#1," for "Ambient Parking #1."

FLASHBACK HOUR

Leaning into the screen, we returned to the emotions of that bygone time. Stirred to the highest pitch of manic jubilation, we longed to stomp onstage like rock stars and smash our guitars to pieces. But seeing as we lacked the necessary charisma, we went out for Chinese food instead.

At a family-style table bedecked with magnum beer bottles and mountains of moo shoo, we twirled the lazy Susan and commemorated our esprit de corps with rhapsodic toasts. "May our productions flourish, our reputations prevail, and our doubters be tormented by the persistent wheezing of a thousand Muzak symphonies!" was how one such tribute went, capped by the festive crashing of glasses. Not to be outdone, the other end of the table issued a rival riposte: "May our descendants be fleet of thought, mighty of heart, and blessed with the assurance that their predecessors lived not as wretched hacks, but as cult figures of the highest caliber and integrity!" Finally, our youngest member stood up on a chair and cleared her throat; the table fell silent. "Down with pretenders, offenders, and false contenders," she cried in a voice quavering with emotion, "and up with the noise of the new sonic revolution!" Deafening roars greeted her pronouncement.

Feverish, we drained our glasses in a single gulp, dashed them impetuously to the ground, and danced a sort of tarantella on the broken shards. Piling into a city bus, we shouted declarations of love for all things bold and beautiful. Within moments, our progress was tied up by a column of double-parked cars. As the bus idled, a platoon of bicyclists rode by in protest of the hegemony of gasoline. Poking our heads out the windows, we cheered hoarsely in support of the two-wheeled activists. As we basked in the ambience of blaring car horns and yelled profanities, the cyclists streamed by en masse, tooting their whistles and ringing their handlebar bells in a show of petrol-free defiance.

Despite a wave of indigestion, our inflated egos impelled us to take on all manner of daring and ill-advised feats. We strolled casually into the middle of a boulevard, halting traffic with outstretched palms. We shimmied up a lamppost and performed chin-ups from the tip of the swooping extension arm. Coming upon a few shiftless characters loitering by a neighborhood corner store, we braced ourselves for an impromptu sparring match. But at the very last moment, we wisely pulled back, for the ruffians were all much bigger and stronger than us. Arriving home, we kicked open the front door, switched on the radio, and danced for three hours straight to a marathon broadcast of 1980s flashback tunes.

The retro mojo of New Wave beats had a salubrious effect. Folding up our arms and striking album-ready poses, we pledged to start work on our full-length collection the next morning. After a late breakfast, we ransacked our residence from top to bottom, knocking down room dividers and converting the bedrooms into a mixing studio. Privacy screens were mounted, the walls soundproofed with sheets of cork and back issues of the *Rolling Stone*. Clothing, bedding, and other remnants of vulgar necessity were relegated to the back storage room. We tiled the floor with reams of musical composition paper, so that we could jot down ideas midstride. Maps were drawn up to chart the development of our motifs from foyer to kitchen, kitchen to bathroom, bathroom to atelier.

It was a time of unparalleled productivity for us. Yet we refrained from overworking our sound, favoring organic spontaneity over fanatical perfectionism. The looseness of our approach kept us open to fresh developments, and our creations gushed forth with all the assurance of an inexhaustible natural resource. We embraced the protean nature of our process. When drowsiness set in, we let our heads drop and arranged melodies from deep within the REM state. When friends stopped by unannounced, we brewed a pot of tea and incorporated the conversation into our background palette. Whispered confidences led to social breakdown, as we layered tracks of gossip over the recorded collisions of bicyclists with taxicab doors, truckers with garage overhangs.

Long walks became customary during this period of growth and increased personal awareness. We would hit the pavement at two-thirty, armed with parasols and hummus sandwiches, and stay out until the heat of the day melted into a pale crimson glow. Unlike previous field trips, these sojourns took on the character of a pilgrimage. We were moving toward a sense of simplicity, the firm resolve of the devoted. Gesturing solemnly, we strolled like free disciples through the city streets, our invisible robes swishing aside dented cans and collected debris. We began to speak of the future in softened tones, as if it were a lost child in need of our care and protection. When approached for spare change, we would stop in our tracks, lower our heads, and turn out our pockets with penitent alacrity.

Each walk was governed by a devotional theme, revealed to us at day's end by the path we had trodden. "Perseverance" pushed us to scale roadblocks and ford canals of untreated water, while "Quietness" took us to the edge of a ballpark, its rows of empty white bleachers overlooking a theater of stillness. "Patience" found us waiting beneath a solitary pine tree for a storm to let up, while "Mindfulness" smacked our foreheads as we leaned in to examine the ornamental woodwork of a swinging door.

One evening, our meanderings brought us to a lane snaking uphill to a neighborhood of three-story Victorians and shiny luxury automobiles. As residential income levels rose, so did the delicacy of our responses. The usual resistances of life seemed to fade away and a note of refinement drifted into our consciousness. Instead of cursing to express displeasure, we arched our eyebrows and flared our nostrils with pregnant meaning. Mild summer breezes brushed across wind chimes in well-kept topiary gardens, soothing our habitual restlessness. We trespassed across a velvety front lawn to a teak gazebo and gazed at the lights of the metropolis below, our eyes glistening meritoriously from our elevated view.

Our attempts to set these walks and their themes to music met with mixed success. In "Serendipity," we introduced felicitous banjo pluckings into the score. But "Foresight" fell flat on its face in the studio, its sweeping vision crumpling beneath the weight of our machine-sequenced bass line. Finally, "Expectation" confounded us with its procession of high-spirited major sevenths followed by a steady descent into gothic gloom.

For weeks, we straddled the fine line between pagan pleasure and funereal excess, cultivating dark eye circles and exploring the emotional nuances of shades of black. When one of us was taunted by the mainstream, we quickly formed a circle of protection around the victim, holding up the fluted arms of our dark coats like enormous bat wings, and stared down the bullies until they slunk away. Gathering up the folds of our raiment, we headed to one of the cavernous lairs that welcomed and nurtured our kind. We sublimated our complex inner world into formidable makeup jobs and swayed ponderously to the gong-based drone. The night drew close around us. We gothed together and were not alone.

A syncopated attack squad of amped-up guitars interrupted our trance and reawakened our punk edge. We confined our repertoire to two power chords, which we played forward and backward, inverted and note by note. We shouted along to the bam-bam beat until our voices grew hoarse and our ears started ringing. Fed up with the status quo, our female members devised a set of riot-grrrl cheers to mock paleo-fascist macho privilege. A posse of men in the audience retaliated and a confused slugfest broke out. Ideological insults ripped through the air amidst a backdrop of swinging microphone stands and overturned drums. Our viola de gamba was smashed, our harpsichord unstrung by wrathful combatants. When the police showed up to drag us away, we dug in our heels and listened for the final traces of ambience emerging from the mayhem.

Much to our surprise, an airy melody floated out from the melee, prompting us to retire our combat boots and reinstate the disco ball. Casting smoldering looks at the audience, we came to deliver vocal renditions of our oeuvre in a breathless falsetto. We grew our hair out in earnest, feathering it into memorable coiffures that were instantly recognizable in silhouette. With our pant hems let out, we sashayed across the dance floor and boogied all night under gyrating spotlights. During this period of one-night stands and short-term love affairs, much sleep was lost and many tears flowed down mascara-streaked faces. But we could always rely on the animal magnetism of our prowling strut, which sprang from the soles of our feet and angled up through our hips like lightning, culminating in a come-hither head turn of tousled tresses. On our days off, we linked arms and went roller skating up and down the waterfront, aligning our terry-cloth wrist bands in a show of rainbow-colored solidarity.

Over time, our most impressionable members dropped analog tuning in favor of the synthesizer, while the exhibitionists among us stepped into the vinyl jumpsuits of nocturnal electro-glam. These two camps took off in separate orbits, only to be reunited in a notorious cabaret where the chanteuses wore satin bustiers and crooned lullabies inspired by the novels of Djuna Barnes. Enticing fragments of conversation wafted over from nearby tables, intermingled with talk of antiessentialism and the Situationist International. Dusky-eyed barmaids carried jewel-toned cocktails across the room and our couch seemed to levitate in zero-gravity splendor. Sadly, we would awaken from these bacchanals to find ourselves back on the mean streets of New York or Los Angeles, rubbing our eyes balefully and groping about for coffee and cigarettes.

During the day, we emulated the dispassionate poise of vampires and zombies, averting our eyes from the sight of mere mortals. As darkness settled, we would reanimate, rising to new heights of guitar strumming and solos suspended in the upper registers. To commemorate our glam-disco-punk phase, we directed a trilogy of Super 8 shorts in which we starred as languid robots in search of free love, backed by a supporting cast of cybernauts and dedicated cosmeticians. At a midnight fundraising event, the films were projected onto the concrete wall of a freeway overpass, where an audience gathered to gawk at the outsized spectacle of our faces plastered in metallic makeup, glaring with haughty disdain at the hastily retreating tail lights overhead.*

---

* All across the city, billboard campaigns depicting massive consumer products had sprung up to compete boundlessly in the free market. Out of sheer necessity, we learned to tolerate the sight of soda cans bigger than Toyotas, khaki cargo pants billowing like sails over high rises. At a popular offramp leading to City Hall, an apartment complex featuring a deluxe billboard sponsored by the cattle industry began to offer penthouses at lowered rates, such that residents now peered out from balconies directly above an airbrushed slab of top sirloin. Visitors could be seen clambering up the service ladder and disappearing behind the garnish on the dinner plate. These developments turned our stomachs and drove us deeper into despair. Unable to locate any meaningful reflections in the skyscape, we built our own altars, our own images of worship. Reckless and unabashed, we resurrected our own faces.

LOOPS AND RAMBLINGS

An untimely fall from ill-fitted platform shoes brought our party career to an end. The patterns of dots and loops on our evening wear accentuated our transformation into human dominos, as we reached out to a neighbor for support only to topple to the ground in swift succession.

Immobilized by leg splints and painkillers, we hired fawning interns from the art institute to fluff up our pillows and cook us comfort food. In return, they earned two units of independent study each, along with bragging rights on the fringe gallery circuit. Whenever we had an immediate medical need or spasm of self-doubt, an intern would appear close at hand to take our temperature and allay our panic. Their constant coddling nurtured us and we often composed spontaneously, dictating radical new harmonies and backbeats while our assistants annotated our notebooks accordingly. Propped up on swiveling Barcaloungers with our palms cupped around steaming bowls of macaroni and cheese, we sighed approvingly as the interns steered vacuum cleaners throughout the flat and indexed our recordings by geographical source and date of inception.

As our health improved, we ventured outside weekly to take in the fresh air and bask in the lengthening rays of autumn. Charming disputes erupted between our caretakers as they fought for the privilege of escorting us on these outings. To support our first steps, the victors would square their shoulders and grip us securely around the middle when we faltered. Anticipating our fatigue, they commandeered a fleet of pull-wagons into which they bundled us, semirecumbent and happily medicated, for the extended trip throughout the city. When the wagon supply dwindled as a result of a toymakers' strike, rolling laundry carts made for a tolerable, if less dignified, alternative. With our interns panting and perspiring to propel the convoy forward, we exercised our wanderlust in spite of our painful injuries.

Once the flat was sufficiently clean, we assigned the interns a more challenging project to help them in their transition to the real world as artists. Their first task was to hook up a new computer donated to us by an anonymous patron of the arts. Next, we plied them with several digital cameras discovered between the couch cushions after a past rave and requested that they take stylish photos of us from the waist up, until our legs were fully recuperated. The images would be posted on a new fan site dedicated to our band, which the interns would be able to claim, in all honesty, to have developed on their own. After downloading the photos to the computer, the interns clicked and dragged diligently, applying filters and twirling images, to digitally enhance unremarkable snapshots of us caught droopy-eyed just before nodding off.

One day, an intern in the midst of surfing the Internet for content to add to the fan site cried out in alarm and waved us over. Gulping down the last of a fruit smoothie, we hobbled over to reassure him as we would a preschooler with his first art project. When we reached the screen, we staggered at the image before us, gripping the desk edge for support as we read the accompanying text. A mediocre jam band who imagined themselves our rivals had sprung up in another part of the state, touring the terrain in an extra-wide pickup truck mounted on lifted shocks and monster tires. An aluminum flagstaff protruded from either side of the cab. On one was hoisted the Stars and Stripes; a skull and crossbones waved piratically from the other.

For weeks, we congregated around the computer to research the other band's exploits, our brows furrowed and our eyes glued to the screen. We assembled this short chronicle of their existence, indisputable evidence of their delusion and conceit, to be included as a supplement to our own manifesto:

Chronicle of the Ambient Barkers

Clambering onto the truck bed with an ice chest of hard lemonade, we pulled up the tailgate and arranged ourselves on milk crates. As we rolled out of the driveway, we headed the wrong way and then executed a screeching U-turn right over the curb and onto our neighbor's pansy garden. We lurched off the sidewalk, jumped the median divider, and barreled down the avenue at top speed, chuckling softly to ourselves as frightened pedestrians leapt out of the way. Whenever an obstacle cropped up in our path, we simply flattened it, leaving dinosaur tread marks crisscrossed over its battered surface.

We exulted in the righteous freedom of our maverick rig. Our single-digit fuel mileage filled us with pride as we pulled into a gas station to top off our tank and defog our windshield. From our elevated perspective, the uniformed attendants were reduced to pipsqueaks, scurrying back and forth with spray bottles and rolls of paper towels. Lowering a rope ladder over our sidewall, we admitted a delegation of quick-mart employees, who hauled themselves up one by one to deliver microwaved miniburgers and nachos into our outstretched hands.

A silvery cloud of exhaust collected around our massive tires, turning the world below us into a liquid mirage. It was a sunny, pitch-perfect day for conducting a citizens' patrol. We divided the city into evenly spaced sectors which we roamed street by street, taking note of landmarks and public establishments where illegal activities might be taking place. Whenever a resident strolled out-of-bounds or seemed otherwise headed for trouble, we sounded our horn, flashed our warning lights, and herded him or her safely back to the mainstream.

Ours was a mandate of national honor and security. Rounding the corner to enter a blighted, underserved community, we slowed to a crawl and tossed handfuls of prescription drugs into the crowd of juveniles who had gathered at our arrival. After a moment's hesitation, they dove after the samples, jostling each other aside to fill their pockets with pills. Only a few hung back with faithless eyes, rejecting our charity out of hand. Ignoring an angry mother who appeared in the street to harangue us, we continued to shower the children with our advanced cure-alls until their scowls turned to silly grins, at which point we closed with a bombardment of religious pamphlets. Mission accomplished, we signaled to our driver to begin evacuation maneuvers.

Order and obedience prevailed under our rule. Wherever we went, heads snapped to attention. Unkempt bohemians slipped their shirts and shoes back on, and public discourse subsided to a discreet murmur. In the dead of night, the homeless were escorted out of the taxpayer's view. In the park, a bull terrier in the midst of relieving itself on a piece of heroic statuary abruptly dropped its hind leg. Throngs of petit bourgeois submitted at once to our authority, in exchange for guaranteed financial freedom and protection. A cadre of muscular, God-fearing youths took to marching in our wake, hailing us with shouts and pumping fists. Touched by their tireless devotion, we blinked back tears and acknowledged their salutes with lightly upraised palms.

Eager to demonstrate our commitment to urban renewal, we soon established a nodding acquaintance with market evangelists, residential developers, and other forward-looking civic leaders. We embarked on a door-to-door outreach campaign in a rent-controlled housing complex, brandishing clipboards with petitions for voluntary self-eviction. When residents declined to sign the statement, copies of the legal memo authorizing our emergency powers were affixed to their doors. At a planning session, we discussed the long-term benefits of building a local detention facility, so that we could seize the heads of household for immediate and indefinite confinement.

Next, we turned our attention to unpatriotic cuisine. Unbeknownst to our leaders and elders, legions of terrorist-friendly foods had crossed the borders undetected and infiltrated the kitchens and lunch counters of our community. The streets were awash in the smells of foreign spices, unleavened breads, couscous, kabobs, and yogurt dips from the axis of garbanzo, coriander, and whey. Even longtime staples of fine European dining could no longer be held above suspicion. After the most recent rounds of parliamentary voting, it was deemed only proper to look askance at plates of paella and greet baskets of shoestring fries with polite but firm refusal.

Those who crossed the fine line of culinary etiquette provoked talk of reeducation. As our special contribution to the effort, we trained teams of youth scouts to operate routine checkpoints where the lunchpails of schoolchildren were inspected for border contamination. Stacks of curried dishes were confiscated, countless pita pockets snatched from the open mouths of babes. One day, we were summoned to the site of a controversy. Our scouts were locked in a standoff with a gang of student activists who were wielding baguettes baked in the shape of peace signs. They were barring our access to a preschooler who was clutching the uneaten portion of an exotic hot dog. A shouting match erupted, followed by a skirmish. Rushing in with a piece of apple pie, we were able to repatriate the child without harm, the bratwurst surrendered into gloved hands.

Despite such easy victories, our campaign was not without its hardships. Loneliness and boredom plagued us, especially when the streets were slow and sleepy and bereft of humanity. Late one Tuesday night, we scanned the radio, stopping when we heard the sounds of an engine winding down, a car door creaking open, and a car alarm sounding. Although we didn't know what the music meant, we set the station to memory, eventually adding the Ambient Parkers to our playlist. Their music initially appealed to us, but always left us wanting more. It was a faint echo of our ramblings: restrained, effete, and unmanly. Heading to a monster truck rally one weekend, we brought along our own recording equipment, which we had used in our efforts to become a teenage speed-metal band. We affixed a microphone to the top of a fence post with Velcro strips and reveled in the sounds of freakish-sized wheels whipping up the dirt, high-riding cabs toppling like felled pines, an unorchestrated series of all-American smack-downs and collisions. Medical personnel carrying kit bags darted across the arena, calling to mind the moving dots on a shooting range.

After hooking up two loudspeakers to the upper rear corners of our cab, we unchained our sound and let it loose on the public like a highly trained mastiff. As we cruised the streets, patrons of outdoor eateries dropped their forks and covered their ears in agony, small children abandoned their toys on front lawns and raced indoors, pampered dogs hearkened to the call of the wild and howled lamentably in our wake. It was a new day, the dawn of Armageddon. The Ambient Barkers had arisen, stoic and battle-ready, determined to triumph in the war over evil.

Satisfied that the evidence we had gathered on the Ambient Barkers would speak for itself, we backed away from the screen, our hair matted and our eyes seared. As we scoured the flat for eye drops, it gradually dawned on us that our real world was in chaos.

While we were consumed by the urgent work of our manifesto, the interns had set up a wireless network in the flat, their laptops in candy colors strewn about on every conceivable surface. In a silent takeover, they had usurped our copyrights and were busy selling our singles at the bargain rate of forty-nine cents apiece over the Internet. One of them even had the nerve to shrug off our outrage as he continued to collect record-low bids from an on-line auction. Taken in by their youthful good looks, we had trusted them implicitly. In this new light, we wondered how we had overlooked their budding capitalist facades. Livid with fury, we bellowed for order, cursing as we overextended the use of our legs.

One by one, they tore themselves away from their screens, lining up against the wall and glaring back at us with callous indifference. At first they gave noncommittal testimony, but a few eventually broke down under pressure to reveal the depths of their infamy. They had sent compromising photos of us to family and friends requesting funds for the care of ailing artists, and pocketed the proceeds. They had tampered with the arrangement of "Ambient Parking #25," layering it over a beat-box routine to form a cheesy Top 40 mix. It now served as the ringtone for their cell phones, which they kept on hand at all times and claimed were generating buzz wherever they went.* Worst of all, they

---

* At city bus shelters, cell phone service providers had begun to plaster their ads, walling in citizens who commuted by transit. No matter where we stood, our gaze fell on images of young models and marketing copy pushing us to stay connected with family and friends. The fine print typically mentioned a minimum two-year contract, monthly payments, and penalties. There was no warning about electromagnetic radiation, nor a mention of the overseas studies correlating frequent use with the development of brain tumors. Whipping out a permanent marker that we carried with us for such occasions, we vandalized one of the ads so that it now read "CONNECTION = DEATH." Our scofflaw act went unnoticed by others at the bus stop who were completely absorbed by their smart phones—talking, texting, checking e-mail, playing video games, browsing digital photos, listening to music downloads, and surfing the Internet.

had snuck out at night and impersonated us in an unauthorized concert, insisting they were safeguarding our fan base during our convalescence. A small but annoying segment of our audience would soon take to heckling us, loudly critiquing our playing and calling for our impostors instead.

Without further delay, we tossed our heartless protégés into the street, where they were quickly reduced to scraping for grant money and tutoring the untalented offspring of millionaires for minimum wage. Meanwhile, we returned to the half-finished recording projects that we had neglected for far too long, taking every precaution to ensure they received our undivided attention. We positioned menacing statuary by our front entrance and installed complicated door locks to discourage ourselves from wandering outside. We set up an autoreply e-mail announcing that we would be away from our inbox for the next thirty years. We disabled our voicemail and limited our phone use to a prearranged hour each week, during which time we would huddle around the receiver and pick up on the first ring.

From the outside, our house resembled an impenetrable fortress, but inside we felt more vulnerable than ever. Daunted by the challenge of generating new work, our minds lost traction and went blank. We shuffled listlessly from room to room, seeking inspiration from drab wall decorations and stale idea boards. During the day, we became addicted to soap operas, talk shows, and high-calorie processed foods. At night, we lost weight from worry, tossing and turning in anticipation of our failure. Like unstable method actors, we watched our bodies balloon to spectacular proportions before shrinking back down to nothing.

In our moments of emaciation, we entertained notions of giving up altogether. We found ourselves daydreaming about death, how pleasant it would be to lie in plush coffins beneath high, rain-glossed windows as our memorial service droned on and on, and a pipe organist played somber renditions of our favorite pop tunes to a handful of mourners. We spent the better part of an afternoon compiling our elegiac playlist for maximum tearjerking effects. Moved to convulsive sobs, we collapsed in a group hug, patting one another in consolation. Later, we came to our senses and felt embarrassed by our self-pity. Dropping to our knees, we pleaded with the gods and demons for the rebirth of our sound.

Finally, we decided that the very notion of inspiration was bankrupt and sought to stimulate production through chance. To shake up our habits, we rolled a handful of dice each morning and used the results to generate chord inversions at the piano. We dusted off our math books and flipped through them, reacquainting ourselves with game theory to explain away the emotional volatility of our practice. We reproduced the stop and go of traffic in our longer sets, patterned after daily fluctuations in the stock market. Through these activities, the illusion of prolific output was created, free from the risks of personal involvement. As our songs seemed to write themselves, our inner selves retreated into hiding, watching and wondering from shelters of cozy detachment.

These procedural techniques, however, could take us only so far, and we found ourselves courting denial. To meet studio deadlines, we concocted potions of liquid courage and fought reality. We padded our chords with proven flourishes and declared the melodies fresh and inspired. We draped our songs in enticing costumes and walked them onto the stage like haute couture. Publicly, we fled to safety zones of twee and distortion; privately, we crumbled in the face of disaster. We cultivated bad moods. We threw childish tantrums without provocation and mumbled sheepish apologies to the floor. We tore up our notebooks and trashed our tapes. We resumed our chain-smoking, secretly delighting as we filled our lungs with noxious fumes. We lived like fugitives in our own home, hunkering down in a different room every night to escape our ruin.

News of our extended convalescence spread far and wide. Before long, family and friends began arriving in shifts to plague us with half-baked casseroles and useless advice. Slumped against our pillows, we listened patiently as one do-gooder extolled the benefits of a high-protein diet, urging us to increase our intake of raw nuts. As a bag of almonds was passed between us, another sat by our bedside and recited passages from a workbook for Christian entrepreneurs. The virtues of hard work and capitalism penetrated our minds like a gospel, shielding our ears from the red-tailed devil who tempted us with the sex and violence of premium cable television. An activist friend beamed with the rewards of nonprofit work, while an author friend presented us with her unpublished manuscript of fables, pressing the creased pages into our palms with a pious, ingratiating smile.

We endured these trials for days, affecting compliance to encourage our houseguests to lose interest and move on. When they showed no signs of leaving, we suddenly declared ourselves healed, jumping out of bed to escort them downstairs. Immediate protests could be heard from all sides. "Do not jeopardize your recovery with such foolishness!" they cried as we thrust their coats at them. "How will you cope without our assistance?" they pleaded as we hustled them through the hall. "Remember your weakened constitutions!" they implored as we pushed them across the threshold. "Call us at the first sign of a relapse!" they conceded at last, as we shut the door behind them. After a few moments of restorative silence, we became aware of our leg muscles, the bittersweet joy of stretching our limbs. We lingered in the foyer and performed sixty-seven jig steps in a row, laughing with pleasure and relief until the blood rushed painfully to our toes.*

Peering into the refrigerator, we realized with a start that it was empty, our misadventures having sapped our emergency funds. Hungry and in need of rent money, we took on a string of odd jobs to make ends meet. We bussed tables and tried in vain to master the espresso machine. We logged hours in the hallowed stockrooms of retail, where we affixed price tags to stacks of identical T-shirts waiting to outfit the youth of America. We lurked by the entrances of boutiques, assaulting weekend shoppers with false cheer and questions about their day. More greeting opportunities arose and we soon found ourselves on familiar terrain, flagging down motorists while wearing sandwich boards and costumes depicting national symbols. Equipped with green foam crowns and torches, we formed a phalanx of welcoming statues in front of an auto dealership, encouraging big-ticket consumerism in support of life, liberty, and the pursuit of happiness.

After weeks of low-paid labor, we abandoned our positions in favor of lucrative white-collar schemes. From the comfort of our own home, we placed cold calls to a list of potential buyers, making slaphappy offers they couldn't refuse. In a friend's basement, we stuffed envelopes for a pyramid operation, promising any takers likely earnings of over fifteen hundred dollars in the first week after a modest opening investment. Near the top of the pyramid, we turned peacefully in our sleep, making money on the global clock as market prices surged from continent to continent. We awoke feeling flush and optimistic, eager to sign in to our on-line brokerage account.

---

* One jig step for every hour of our confinement.

When our speculative profits failed to cover material expenses, however, we fell into massive debt. To pay the bills, we enlisted once again in the workday grind, this time farming ourselves out as copy clerks for the documentation department of a Fortune 500 firm. Although our duties were tedious and mind-numbing, one of our members latched onto his position and surprised us all by ascending the corporate ladder with ease. A sluggish and incompetent worker by nature, he caught the eye of a superior who saw him as a fitting candidate for management. With each new promotion, he acquired more abstract authority and fewer tangible duties. His cryptic facial expressions and ignorance of practical matters produced a disarming aura that blended in perfectly with executive culture. When he finally achieved the corner office with its six-figure salary, we declared him the household breadwinner and submitted our resignations at once.

Our days of leisure were restored. After rolling out of bed at ten-thirty, we made our way to the kitchen for morning coffee and brioche, checking first for signs that our salaryman had left hours earlier and everything was in working order. At six-thirty sharp, he would stumble across the threshold, groaning from the collected burdens of his day. Lying facedown on the couch, he would sigh and emit martyred ululations until one of us pulled off his shoes and administered a stress-relieving backrub. Cigarettes were carefully plucked from a gold case, lit, and placed between his lips. Dry martinis were supplied on demand; on the toughest days, a double whiskey straight with chaser was his refreshment of choice. While he sipped and swirled his drink, we retreated to the kitchen to heat up his supper, which he wolfed down on the couch in front of prime-time programming before passing out from a slew of postprandial beers. Every other week, he would develop a nervous tic and lecture us on the importance of household economizing, as we dropped our dish towels and hung our heads in shame.

Such despotic scenes only inflamed our growing homemakers' unrest. In the mornings, we now spent a good three hours cleaning the house, pausing between tasks to swallow cups of coffee and comb the daily paper for coupons. Lunch was typically a slapdash affair—a bowl of canned soup with buttered toast on the side. Afternoons were dedicated to grocery shopping and other mundane errands about town, after which we convened in the kitchen to prepare the evening meal. The hours slipped by as we toiled to maintain a tidy, functioning home, only to watch the floors attract dust again, the linens pile up in the hamper, the rooms succumb to the daily effects of entropy. During our one free hour before supper, we collapsed on our freshly made beds, too careworn from our repetitive duties to even think of reviewing our recordings or practicing our music.

To make matters worse, our steadfast provider was beginning to act strangely. In contrast to his usual self-sacrificial air, he took to strolling in with bright eyes and an overcaffeinated gait, refusing cocktails and withdrawing to his room. A few minutes before supper he would reappear, plopping down on the couch and humming happy tunes to himself. Our suspicious minds began to tick. After days of receiving dodgy responses to our questions, we hired a private investigator and arranged to have our salaryman followed. The gumshoe tailed him for over a week before compiling this detailed chronicle of his typical workday:

The Salaryman Chronicles

8:20 AM—Subject emerges from front entryway of group residence. Rushes down front steps, only to rush back up after touching hand to forehead. Emerges again from entryway, this time with a slim volume tucked under right arm.

Subsequent inspection through binoculars reveals volume to be a comic book, of the caped superhero and mutant villain variety.

8:23 AM—Subject enters corner bakery. Purchases large to-go drink and pastry. While seated, digests front page of morning paper (approx. 2 min.) and entire contents of comic book (approx. 20 min.).

Later, inquiries made to counter person, who claims subject always orders a large café latte with double shot of espresso and a Swiss twinkie.

8:50 AM—Subject walks briskly to inbound bus shelter. Exchanges pleasantries with fellow commuters. Flirts with shorthaired female wearing culottes, striped knee socks, and platform boots. Upon boarding bus, offers seat to same female and anchors self close-by with overhead strap.

9:17 AM—Bus arrives downtown and subject emerges.

9:20 AM—At entrance to office building, subject hesitates for a moment before bolting to the right. Walks down street, across intersection, and in through doors of large retail electronics store. After perusing aisle of cell phone accessories and idling near battery kiosk, subject proceeds to video gaming section, where he monopolizes the racecar simulator (approx. 35 min.).

10:15 AM—Subject bustles into office building and greets receptionist with jokey right-handed salute. Receptionist laughs obligatorily.

10:19 AM—Subject stops at company-sponsored coffee cart to order midmorning pick-me-up and snack (single macchiato and high-protein energy bar). Initiates social chatter with several upper management types, adjusting face and gestures to match the mood of the moment.

10:58 AM—Subject takes elevator car to seventh floor.

11:02 AM—Subject ducks inside empty cubicle. Cracks open briefcase, takes out stacks of documents, and begins to annotate pages with brows furrowed.

11:09 AM—Subject pushes papers aside and looks disparagingly at pencil tip. Journeys down corridor, past elevators, and down another corridor to office supply room, where he makes use of the electric pencil sharpener and grabs a fistful of pens. Retraces steps back to cubicle, only to discover favorite pen color missing. Journeys again to supply room to take corrective action.

11:21 AM—Becomes fascinated by prominent ink stain on padded wall of cubicle.

11:26 AM—Lifts eyes from work and stares vacantly into air.

11:28 AM—Examines fingernails, and rolls shirt sleeves up and down again.

11:30 AM—Conducts intense hallway conversations with three junior employees who appear to be his direct reports.

11:49 AM—Subject yawns, noticeably fatigued by his managerial duties. Dodges inside elevator car and descends to company cafeteria for early lunch.

11:52 AM—Pauses at company bulletin board to nominate self for employee excellence award.

11:55 AM—Places order at grill (double Angus steak burger with bacon strips and side of garlic fries).

12:01 PM—Subject saunters through dining hall with lunch tray in hand, stopping to accost colleagues with light banter. Interrupts conversation repeatedly to toss greetings to passing acquaintances, attend to alert beeps on cell phone, and wave demonstrably to coworkers seated at far end of hall.

12:33 PM—Subject makes beeline for most popular lunch clique seated at center of dining hall. Plants self at head of table and begins to complain about burger somehow being cold. Slurps down large cola and proceeds to hold forth loudly on one topic after another.

In surreptitious interviews conducted shortly afterward, clique members assume subject is a corporate bigwig based on his meticulous attire and cavalier attitude, despite ignorance of his name or job title.

2:07 PM—Subject jumps up from table in panic and runs toward elevators, remarking to several in passing about a two o'clock meeting. Rushes to designated conference room only to find it empty. Flips on light switch and chooses seat near window, as other stragglers file in from late lunch engagements.

2:13 PM—Two o'clock meeting is finally called to order. Along with eleven other attendees, subject turns toward presentation screen to view various charts, metrics, and forecasts on the corporate value of time. During group discussion, subject zones out and appears to pass into zombielike state. Is recalled to consciousness by arrival of the three o'clock hour, at which point his eyes fly open, exhibiting the unnatural brightness and intensity of a newly wakened amnesiac.

Excerpt from meeting handout is appended to this report.*

---

* *From* "Corporate Time: A Taxonomy"

Company Time—official operating hours to be recorded by Accounting for legal and tax purposes

Company Time Off—official nonoperating hours (i.e., weekends, national holidays, and secularized Christian holidays) to be recorded by Accounting for legal and tax purposes

Commute Time—daily nonoperating time required to transport the labor force from sites of residence to offices of employment, and vice versa

Core Time—mandated working hours, typically Monday through Friday from 9:00 AM to 5:00 PM, for which the Company is legally obligated to provide compensation

Flextime—designated working hours outside of Core Time, for which the Company is legally obligated to provide compensation

Overtime—undesignated working hours outside of Core Time during which deadlines are met, for which the Company may or may not be legally obligated to provide compensation

Personal Time—hours outside of Commute Time, Core Time, Flextime, and Overtime, during which employees may conduct their personal affairs and for which the Company is exempt from providing compensation

3:03 PM—Subject staggers into break room for cup of black coffee. Grimaces upon first sip.

3:05 PM—Subject arrives at darkened window office. After glancing left and right, pushes door open and enters. Flips on

---

Comp Time—compensation for Overtime in the form of paid Personal Time, to be offered verbally without follow-through or rarely

Pro Bono Time—labor performed by student interns, for which the Company is exempt from providing compensation

Global Time—unprecedented round-the-clock productivity made possible by remote offices, virtual communication, and transnational commerce

Productive Time—concentrated bursts of time spent producing measurable and profitable results

Unproductive Time—misuse of Company Time expended on personal activities (e.g., surfing the Internet, phoning third parties, socializing with coworkers outside of team-building activities), for which the Company is unfortunately legally obligated to provide compensation

Breaktime—two mandated fifteen-minute breaks set aside for employee bathroom runs, for which the Company is exempt from providing compensation

Lunchtime—mandated nonworking hour typically at noon and set aside for employee meal consumption, for which the Company is exempt from providing compensation

Vacation Time—mandated nonworking hours, typically eighty hours per year, granted and paid for by the Company; employees are expected to increase their Productive Time before and after Vacation Time to minimize its impact on the Company

Ramp-up Time—hours spent training employees to perform their responsibilities to the Company, for which the Company is unfortunately legally obligated to provide compensation

Downtime—periods of slowdown in business activity characterized by surges in Unproductive Time, for which the Company is unfortunately legally obligated to provide compensation

Sick Time—hours of unplanned illness confirmable by a Company-sponsored physician, for which the Company is unfortunately legally obligated to provide compensation

Hardship Time—extended hours of unplanned illness, family emergency, or bereavement during which Personal Time encroaches upon Company Time, thereby posing an irremediable hardship on the Company

Dead Time—hours definable neither as Company Time nor Personal Time, Productive Time nor Unproductive Time, during which an employee has come to an untimely end, thereby posing an immediate quandary for Janitorial Services and Human Resources light switch and raises window blinds. Adjusts seat height, lumbar support, and armrests of Herman Miller Aeron chair. Leans back in chair and swivels in semicircular arc, gazing down through window at ant-sized people below.

3:08 PM—Powers on computer, cracks open briefcase, and spreads papers out on desk.

3:11 PM—Yawns and makes listless attempts to commence work.

3:15 PM—Subject tilts head back, curls upper lip, and places pen between curled lip and nostrils. Pen drops to floor. Subject picks up pen and repeats exercise.

3:24 PM—In response to shuffling noise heard in hallway, subject hastily switches off lights, pulls plug on computer, and dives under wood-paneled desk. Remains in hiding place as company security guard strolls past darkened office, around corner, and out of sight.

3:25 PM—Emerges from concealment, visibly flustered.

3:33 PM—Subject restores office to working condition. In burst of extreme productivity, composes long e-mail summarizing main takeaway points of time management summit. Generates twenty-page slide-show presentation based on same.

4:21 PM—Energized and exultant, subject rides elevator car down to lobby and exits building in search of reward. Walks two blocks north and one block west to arrive at main entrance of upscale shopping mall.

4:28 PM—Subject weaves through shoppers to gourmet food court, where reward is promptly had (large café americano and fresh vanilla bean cream puff). Sits in booth, sipping and munching contemplatively.

4:40 PM—Subject meanders into retail store specializing in high-tech luxury gadgets. Examines instant champagne chiller and tries out portable putting green. Eases into massage chair and experiments with controls on handheld remote.

4:47 PM—Midway through automated program, subject glances over to discover coworker similarly reclined on neighboring massage chair. Vibrating therapeutically in tandem, subject and neighbor exchange office gossip and compare notes on shared struggles with work-related stress.

5:03 PM—Stretching newly loosened muscles, subject strolls back to work, only to meet a profusion of employees just exiting building. Promptly turns on heel and joins throngs of workers headed homeward.

5:10 PM—Waits at corner for outbound bus, whistling brightly and tapping right foot.

A sheaf of dismal photographs accompanied the investigative report, depicting the subject in various postures of idleness. Quietly seething, we closed up the folder. Two days later, our salaryman arrived home to find us awaiting him in a circle of confrontation. Within a week, he was stripped of his breadwinner privileges and forced to assume the lion's share of household chores. In a dramatic coup d'état, we demanded that he fetch our slippers and serve us home-cooked meals nightly. On Saturday afternoons, we lounged in our bathrobes with open boxes of bonbons and glasses of white wine, as he trudged back and forth between home and the Laundromat, lugging unwieldy hampers and jugs of color-safe bleach.

Shortly thereafter, a report addendum arrived from the private investigator, revealing that our salaryman's position at the company had, in fact, been eliminated one month earlier. Through a tacit arrangement based on pity, he was permitted to squat in the office building on weekdays, continue his redundant duties, and collect dwindling severance pay. While he updated his résumé and paraded himself before Human Resources, we sharpened our penny-pinching skills, trading our high-rent flat for a noisome residential suite nestled in the armpit of the city.

Our new neighborhood was a veritable cornucopia of toxic fumes and waste. Pungent odors wafted up from the sewers and a greasy residue oozed from the open pores of building facades. Our nightly quests for cheap entertainment left us unsatisfied, prompting us to dig up our old tapes and reconnect with the degradations of our art. Inspired by a street fight, we composed wordless anthems in praise of vicious youth and dirty glamour. When our worship morphed to annoyance, we embarked on a community outreach program, hoping to gather sympathizers to our cause. To attract other penurious artists, we began to host evenings of free music and light refreshment, followed by artistic discussions on our living room floor. Fueled by salty pretzels and malt liquor, these gatherings sometimes grew heated as rival aesthetes hurled pedantic arguments at one another before a salon party of intoxicated spectators.*

Revitalized by our involvement in the community, we pushed on with the shaping of our album, making strides with new and remixed work. Like parasites, we attached ourselves to the flanks of the professional music scene, sucking out the vital nutrients required to build our careers. Influential connections were established, valuable contacts sustained through special favors and routine flattery. At the cutting edge of culture, we scanned the underground media for ideas, appropriating the latest styles

---

* Oddly, these gatherings took on a religious quality and we began to approach them as church functions, where our simple attendance fulfilled a deep moral obligation and confirmed our inherent superiority. The artists wandered the city streets in tight clusters like members of an obscure ideological sect. As initiates, we learned to display our piety by rejecting secular concerns such as the pursuit of money and personal grooming. We watched as newcomers were scolded and then ostracized for offenses such as flaunting worldly goods or painting their faces like prostitutes. On weekends, we frequented the Salvation Army in search of used clothing that was noticeably battered or stained. When breaking bread with fellow artists, we were careful to uphold the beliefs of the community, hesitant to speak out lest we be branded infidels.

and trends into our work. Following feuds and scandals in the music community with calculated interest, we boosted up the winners with hyperbolic praise and snubbed the losers with great disdain.

Soon we began to emulate the best mudslingers in town, basking in the attention garnered by our gratuitous spew. Whenever we felt low or insecure about our work, we took a poke at our more successful colleagues, forcing them to defend their reputations and answer to trivial points of criticism. Such competitive exploits enlivened us at first, but proved detrimental in the long run. We hung back at group events, propped up in a dingy corner near the lavatory or supply closet. Friends telegraphed their support with long-distance waves and fist bumps, dropping our connection whenever a third party drew near. We turned to our longtime fans, only to find that they too looked uneasy in our presence. Chastened, we holed up in our slumdog suite, vowing to reemerge only after shedding our overbearing ways.

The days passed with frightful monotony. We sought consolation in our extensive record collection, but the albums that had once given voice to our most ardent feelings now struck us as childish and stale, as if by overplaying them through the years we had pressed traces of our past selves onto the vinyl, engraving our most unflattering aspects into the grooves. It could be torture to hear certain songs, or even just catch a hint of them in the background, and be reminded of our tremulous youth, our starry-eyed aspirations, our mortifying teenage crushes, our midnight cruising up and down the main drag.

Other songs threw us into turmoil, like an older sister parading her superior tastes and experiences. A few notes could return us to our slack-jawed adoration for all things wild and extravagant: our ornamental tortoiseshell spectacles, our first of many black berets, our exaltation of the Beats, our deification of Jean Seberg, our wistful attachment to Francois Truffaut, our memorization of manifestos from *Cahiers du Cinéma*, our breathless quotation of these same passages to peers, our unconsummated love for Mirelle Matthieu, our lip-sync tributes to Johnny Mathis, our dialectical struggles with Bob Dylan, our deadpan emulations of the Velvet Underground, our air-guitar journeys with Jimi Hendrix, our slavish imitations of Roxy Music, our sonic make-out sessions with Prince.

The radio offered fresh alternatives. We became aficionados of a pirate station that showcased archival recordings of brilliant but neglected musicians, broadcasting from a different undisclosed location every week to escape federal regulation. It soon became our dearest ambition to achieve airtime on this channel, despite the station master's violent contempt for our genre. We bombarded him with greetings, freebies, and self-promotional fliers, his numerous rebuffs only strengthening our desire to prove ourselves to him. We tracked his schedule of public appearances, following him to interviews and conferences in a grand gesture of admiration that fell somewhere between infatuation and stalking. We sat in the front row along with others in the grip of his cult charisma, trying in vain to catch his eye, win his approval, or even be the target of one of his withering critiques.

Eventually, we established a means of correspondence, in which we offered a supportive ear in exchange for his rants and diaristic grumblings. In the midst of his curmudgeonly messages, he would drop occasional nuggets of advice and reveal the philosophy behind his radio programming in the form of parenthetical confessions and touching asides. We continued to respond in earnest, fostering his trust with our unwavering acceptance, until he finally let loose and bared his soul to us in a torrent of uncensored feeling and abuse. "Friends, you have vastly overestimated your talents," he fired at us from a pseudonymous e-mail account. The hefty note went on.

THE STATION MASTER

Friends, you have vastly overestimated your talents. The artists I promote have a steadfast, practically religious commitment to their music. They always show up on time and they never whine, playing their hearts out with plain and terrifying conviction. Your demo tape, by contrast, reveals that you are technically untrained and more interested in the impossibility of your sound than the honest, backbreaking labor required to achieve it. Your style is derivative and weak. Your laziness shows. I regret to inform you that my computer plays the guitar better than any of you ever could. What you've created here isn't music. At best, it's a representation of music, a conceptual trick, a pathetic substitute for the real thing.

As you can tell, my opinion of your experiments (if "opinion" is the correct term for the feeling that has just come over me, disrupting my composure and afflicting my bowels with a peculiar burning sensation) is far from sanguine. Though I consider myself a modern male with left-of-center values and fearless metrosexual leanings, your swishy avant-pop sensibilities never fail to give me the willies. Your heroic posturing, embellished with fortissimo cadenzas and velvet-pawed escapes into the drapery folds of a nineteenth-century drawing room, makes me writhe with the heebie-jeebies. Pray do not ask me to inflict such crap on my listeners, who have never asked for anything more than an audible resting spot for their troubles, a well-crafted hook to hang their emotions on.

Nevertheless, your persistent stream of unsolicited MP3s does inspire a kind of wonder. I must confess to an idle, even affectionate curiosity about your motives, much as one might feel moved to engage an amiable, somewhat mentally challenged stranger in conversation, if only to experience the momentary balm of human contact. It's with such occasional bonhomie that I feel the core of my being softening. My judgment relaxes and I no longer feel the same resistance to the strangeness of your sound. After all, we are united, are we not, in this campaign of daily toil and invisible striving, fueled solely by our faith in a listenership that might give our efforts the proper consideration? "Is this noise really so intolerable?" I ask myself, lowering my headphones as a light breeze lifts the curtain from my window sill, brushing away the flecks of tobacco ash dropped there by one of my thoughtless visitors.

I turn again to the photograph you sent me, a portrait of your band "in transition," as you were so careful to explain in your cover letter. The lighting, of course, is atrocious and the composition out of kilter. In an effort to achieve a grainy, art-book effect, your photographer used high-speed black and white, which, despite looking pretentious, offers the happy side benefit of obscuring your unappealing features. Most of your members are out of focus and looking away from the camera. They look less like a band than a random assortment of people chasing unrelated goals and having just stumbled into the frame by accident. Several appear to be unaware of the camera altogether, although their freshly mussed hairdos and exaggerated pensiveness makes it obvious that their indifference is strictly an act. A young man in the back has his mouth strangely pursed or bunched to one corner in a disconcerting manner. He appears to have discovered a morsel of food between his teeth and is dislodging it by sucking in his cheeks to create a vacuum. His eyes are focused inward, as if he's mentally going over his last meal in an effort to identify the mysterious tidbit. Perhaps he's even marveling at the boundless capacity of living things to generate and store their own foodstuffs—from the sun-kissed sugars coursing through the xylem and phloem of woody plants to the mashed-up seeds and worms regurgitated into the gullets of baby birds by their doting parents, and now this gem made possible by sloppy oral hygiene. Of course, this spectacle does little to improve the general appearance of your band, whose members are, if nothing else, united in their homeliness. It's only my considerable fortitude and humanitarian resolve that enables me to view this array of greasy forelocks, unibrows, and scrawny necks without succumbing to nausea or bolting from the room in alarm. The sole exception is that fellow near the front, the rakishly handsome youth with the peaked cap who gazes steadily into the camera as if to say, "Admire me, judge me, revile me, it's all the same. For with this face and these pecs, I shall conquer all and never look back." Alas, is he by chance the one who recently renounced Ambient Parking altogether to pursue a more credible line of work? Pizza delivery, was it? Or male modeling? I can't say that I blame him.

But you should know by now that I speak derisively only when I wish, on some secret level, to speak tenderly. All at once, as I put on my headphones and surrender to your noise, I find myself in a state of confusion, groping my way through the landscape of incoherent sounds that I roamed in my youth. I remember them well, my travels! I was a naive young man when I decided to pack up my possessions and see the world. Fresh out of the music conservatory, I set off at once for the nearest metropolis, where I was nickel-and-dimed for every thinkable expense and promptly seduced by a coloratura soprano fourteen years my senior. She installed me in her upper-story rooms as her live-in accompanist after my landlord (that flatulent bastard) evicted me for running the hot water tap too long and too often. (And just how did he expect me to warm up my hands in that frigid excuse of a studio?) In my lover's rooms, I fared much better, at least initially. Annika paid for everything, leaving me free to devote the greater part of each day to my own projects. I would practice the arpeggione. Or I would review the various symphonic transcriptions of Brian Wilson and Lennon/McCartney tunes that I was devising with a partner from the opposite coast, and hoped to market someday as relaxing mood music for business hotels throughout Eastern Europe and Asia. My only real duty was to look after Annika's lapdog, an aging Bichon Frise named Malvolio—to stuff him with frivolous treats and take him on walks along the grass-covered traffic island outside our building.

In our apartment, there was no thought of banalities like water conservation. I could fill the entire Jacuzzi with steaming hot water if I liked, plunge my arms in all the way to my shoulders, and bask in the play of jets streaming against my fingers and palms, massaging the joints and ligaments awake. When at last I removed my hands, they tingled with an electric, practically obscene energy. I would towel off straight away, reach for my instrument and bow, and ravish Schubert's sonata with intensity and fervor. When Annika returned in the evening, I would switch to the baby grand and play accompaniment while she rested her hand on the piano shelf and sang for the intimate circle of financiers and dilettantes whom we entertained on a regular basis. Or I would escort her to one of her performances, waiting faithfully by the stage door as she emerged into a throng of protégés and admirers, her bare shoulders draped in lamé, her cheeks still flushed from the exhilaration of her recent arias. An armful of bouquets accepted, a few autographs signed in an airy hand, and we'd be off in a sable Town Car, headed toward Enrico's, Scarlatti's, Brunnhilde's, or any one of the lively establishments that served midnight plates and cocktails to the operatic set. Soon after our arrival, we would be surrounded by a jovial crowd of conductors, musicians, scenic and costume designers, and fellow singers who hailed the waiter, ordered rounds of champagne, passed platters of oysters back and forth, congratulated one another with hugs and kisses, boasted, gossiped, cackled, and scolded Annika for bringing me, a mere boy musician, to such a place of theatrical debauchery. This last remark was usually accompanied by a tipsy wink or pinch to my cheek, as if I were an overgrown infant out past his bedtime. Then the table would ring with peals of laughter, no one seeming to notice my teeth gritted in rage or that the joke had gotten stale ages ago. "Don't fret, my darling," Annika would whisper, cradling her braceleted arm around my shoulder. "It's only their way of showing you affection. You must not take it to heart." Then turning to her neighbor on the other side, she would resume her anecdote about the hypochondriac composer from Prague or the stammering baritone from Palermo who was infatuated with her, and try in vain to draw me into the fun.

Yes, I endured these indignities because I loved her, just as I endured her numerous dalliances and infidelities, at least the ones I knew about. I could hardly bear the thought of the ones I wasn't aware of or only suspected. There were the accompanists, of course—those practice-room Romeos, those degenerate keyboard flunkeys named Wilmer or Ichiro who wore pomade in their hair and carnations in their buttonholes, and praised her lavishly after every pretty run of notes in the upper registers. And the guest conductors and visiting artistic directors who asked—no, begged—for her attendance at private after-hours rehearsals and late-night tête-à-têtes. It was imperative, they'd say, to rehearse a daring modification to the score or a subtle change in the emphasis placed on the closing note of a tragic soliloquy. Over a special nightcap, they'd command her to repeat the phrase over and over until the expression was just right and to the maestro's liking, always demanding more and more from her, until at last, after god knows how many sessions of breathless, passionate *labor*, she was allowed—no, ordered— to return home. She would enter the apartment chattering incoherently (it was four in the morning by now and I'd been waiting up for hours) about what a genius the maestro was, how inspired his interpretations were, the sensitivity of his hands, his miraculous artist's hands, as I helped her out of her coat and tried not to notice her disheveled hair, trembling shoulders, and face infused with such a look of sublime bliss that I felt torn between a maddening jealousy and a maddening desire to throw her down on the couch and make love to her on the spot. But Annika, sensing my madness, would put up a protesting hand and turn away like a true bel canto heroine, explaining that she was due in for a dress rehearsal at ten in the morning and needed her beauty rest.

One evening, after leaving Annika in the company of a tenor, basso buffo, and mezzo-soprano known for her enthusiastic interpretations of Early Music trouser roles, I decided to forego the usual cab ride and walk home instead. It was a warm night and a balmy, almost subtropical breeze wafted across the sidewalk as I began navigating the twenty or so blocks uptown. I lost myself in the shop window displays, gawking at the various designer suits I could never afford on the measly monthly allowance from my trust fund. The weather had roused the romantic impulses of my fellow city dwellers, evidenced by the steady stream of couples who walked hand in hand through the streets, monopolizing the sidewalks with their oblivious, self-consumed joy. At times I had to hop nimbly between parking meters or into the gutter to avoid colliding with them. After several such encounters, I decided I'd had enough and ducked into a side alley leading to a low-rent neighborhood dotted with packs of adolescents, street pushers, and beat-up cars. I was hungry, and it was the perfect time to eat something that Annika and her set would wrinkle their noses at. Tempted by the greasy smell of fast food, I stopped in at a place on the corner for a corn dog and soda. As I chewed and slurped, I thought of the scene I'd just left. I recalled the gaudy yet undeniably pricey decor of

Brunnhilde's—the scarlet divans with heart-shaped backs and oversized nailhead trim, the horned helmets suspended high over the heads of patrons on translucent wires like an apocalyptic ghost army. I remembered Annika's face when I stood up from the bar to go—that too bright and too easily animated face—how she had waved good night to me a bit too readily and drunkenly, instructing me to feed Malvolio a liver pill before going to bed. I thought too of her three companions (those vocal parasites) who had stared at me coolly as I withdrew, seizing their opportunity to close in on my mistress with alarming swiftness, especially the mezzo in Baroque costume who was a real swaggering über-dyke—pressing his/her slippered foot against Annika's gilded sandal, sliding his/her lace-cuffed arm around Annika's waist, lowering his/her dandified curls to whisper into Annika's ear.

I recalled the episode with much bitterness and would have continued in this vein indefinitely, dwelling on key moments to stoke the embers of my misery, but the time had come for me to vacate my booth. Two shifty-eyed strangers were staring in my direction, one sporting a baseball cap and slurping a milkshake, the other wearing a ski cap and conveying fistfuls of French fries to his mouth. Both were looking me up and down menacingly, with special attention to my gold-plated watch and ivory opera scarf. After gnawing off the last morsels of deep-fried cornmeal from the stick, I made a dash for the exit. By weaving through the sidewalk crowd erratically, I was soon able to shake off the thugs. A wise voice inside me reminded me to yank off my scarf and watch, and stuff them inside my waist pocket. In a grimy storefront window, I caught a glimpse of my reflection: crazy eyes, lips caked with burnt crumbs, and bulging jacket front. I was beginning to feel a little crazy all over. My arms pumped like pistons, churning the warm air around me. My stride opened up and my steps grew increasingly defiant. I was beginning to feel at home among all the slackers, pushers, and pimps, as if the mere fact of my rejected existence amounted to an initiation into the seamy underworld. My transformation was accepted by the locals without question; people either skipped off to the side as I approached or nodded to me respectfully. Elaborate fantasies began to creep into my mind. I thought of changing my name, setting up shop in this neighborhood where nobody knew me, and disappearing altogether. Or I would put on a dark suit and join one of those itinerant bands that marched in the wake of funeral processions, playing slow, solemn dirges. Yes, I thought as the steam vents opened up around me and expelled gusts of hot air, I would soon make a new life for myself. Suddenly a low boom echoed through the street. People began to run in all directions, a few toward the source of the disturbance. I floated past all the chaos like a cabin cruiser. Sirens picked up force in the distance, a car alarm began to wail, and I felt deliriously happy. Happy, happy!

My flight of fancy vanished, however, as soon as I reached the entrance to my building and recognized the mournful face of the night doorman. He looked over my disheveled appearance and held open the door without comment. In the darkness of the empty apartment, all my loneliness returned with a vengeance. I flicked on the kitchen light and poured myself a highball of whiskey. Malvolio jumped off his pillow by the fireplace and pattered over to me, looking for attention. I pushed him firmly away and then walked over to the piano with my drink and raised the lid. My fingers found E-flat minor and I started to play, improvising moody chords that melted and collapsed into one another, a mass of crumpled sounds tripping forward without rhyme or reason. All the notes blurred into one as I gulped down the last of my bitter drink.

Later, as Malvolio lay stretched out in my lap, accepting the nightly brush strokes that Annika insisted were necessary for the health of his coat, I spoke out loud: "You and I are the same, my friend. We are afterthoughts, afterthoughts and captives here in this apartment, where everything seems to be at our disposal, everything except the one thing or person we really need, who only takes notice of us when it's convenient for her." As I spoke, I gazed into Malvolio's round, limpid eyes and lapsed into a trance of self-pity. Sensing my distraction, the dog jumped out of my lap and trotted away to bury his snout in his food dish. The sight of this pampered, not too bright animal, slurping up mouthfuls of food and flinging sprays of half-chewed kibble joyfully left and right, made my heart sink. A surge of indignation arose in me and I drew myself up to full height. What had happened to my life? Where was my pride? I vowed to reclaim my manhood in the only way that mattered, through the complete and unequivocal mastery of my instrument. I decided to try an infamous finger-strengthening exercise favored by the old Romantic players. With a strip of coarse linen, I fastened the third and fourth fingers of my fretting hand together. Then I raised my instrument to my knees and rehearsed an exceptionally difficult passage with some very fast chromatic runs. I played the eight bars over and over again, taking pains to clearly articulate the notes corresponding to the third finger while omitting the notes corresponding to the fourth. Then I loosened the bandage, retied it around my fourth finger and pinkie, and repeated the exercise, which according to legend would restore my virtuoso technique. Already I could feel the power returning to my hand, an exhilarating force coursing through my veins. I poured myself another highball and practiced late into the night, until my muscles were exhausted. When Malvolio interrupted me with his yapping, I fed him his liver pill and topped off his water bowl with the last of the whiskey. Then I gave myself a double shot of vitamin B and climbed into bed.

I can't remember when Annika finally got home. It might have been half past five, but it might have been earlier or later, the exact hour being hard to judge in my state of nervous intoxication. I do know that I awoke to a wounded red dawn pushing in through the curtains and the dim outline of Annika rummaging through the top drawer of her dresser for a sleep mask. What happened next? I believe I must have charged at her. It shames me to say it, but tears may have been shed, tears of rage and of a terrible foreboding. I was absolutely beside myself, a pathetic mess, yet—I believe you will understand me when I say this—I also felt acutely alive, a man confronting a lonely and indifferent world, the hero at last of my own hapless story. Annika stared at me, her face a mixture of awe, fear, and contempt for what I had become. Her body swayed slowly, and for a minute it looked as if she might collapse. Then she collected herself, and with a studied effort, she threw her head back and laughed. It was a high, musical laugh, not quite cruel but certainly practiced, a laugh that uncorked itself with a pop and bubbled upward in rapidly ascending cadences, ornamented with skips, leaps, and pretty little trills—the effervescent laughter of Violetta tossing all cares away in the face of life's countless pleasures, the pitiless laughter of Adina mocking the foolish passion of simpletons, the triumphant laughter of the Queen of Night reveling in the magical forest. In short, it was a laugh that was the last best defense of a proud woman caught off guard, which Annika certainly was—her hair in disarray, her dress wrinkled and reeking of smoke (imported cigarettes being the vice of choice for reckless divas who liked to gamble with their vocal cords), her sandals kicked off to a corner with one strap hanging loose, one heel missing. I had caught her when she least expected it. Or perhaps (it flashed upon me in a moment of insight) I had caught her at the only time possible, this train wreck of a meeting being the one inevitability that we could have arrived at by amoral design. Annika had been waiting weeks, possibly months, for me to confront her in precisely this way, just as I had been crawling bit by bit my entire lifetime toward this moment of truth. Thoughts went round and round in my head. It seemed unthinkable for me to leave Annika, just as it did for Annika to admit her unhappiness with our domestic arrangement and kick me out. I searched my mind frantically for a solution, some way out of this vicious cycle of jealousy and recrimination, some way to stop the false laughter pouring out of Annika's mouth.

I gripped the edge of the vanity table for support, my knees buckling. For a second, I thought I saw two Annikas: the one exhausted, guilty, and ready to give up the game; the other haughty, controlled, and indecisive, unable to embrace me or let me go. A heavy feeling of loss welled up in my chest. I thought back to the early days of our romance, when a very different song had been sung, a song that rivaled the very best of Puccini's arias with its emotive depths and rich melody—reaching out and questioning, yearning, advancing to climaxes of joy, then pausing to catch its breath, dipping down just a little to reconsider its purpose before pivoting, leaning wholeheartedly into a breathless sigh. The laughter had stopped and Annika looked at me, saying nothing. In my despair, I read her silence as repudiation, as confirmation of how stupid I had been to imagine myself the intended recipient of her song (for it seemed only fitting now to describe the song as originating from her and her alone; I could hardly call it our song anymore!). In my mind's wanderings, she was showing me my proper place at the end of a long line of suitors, where I was always a stand-in, never a favorite. My heart sank, my body went limp, and I steeled myself for the long miserable walk through the miserable city streets, back to my miserable hole of a studio with its miserable lukewarm plumbing. I realized then that I couldn't leave her and I consoled myself with an elaborate fantasy: I was just about to reach for my coat when Annika stirred. "Darling," she beckoned. I watched her lips move, banishing the silence, dispelling my fears with the bare simplicity of her voice. She paused to take a breath, and I thought I could hear an orchestra building slowly at her feet: first the cellos and violas commencing in a soft pianissimo, next the flutes and violins joining in the tremolo, and then all the strings and woodwinds mounting together to support her, as she stepped forward to test the growing power of her voice. Her resolution strengthened with each new crescendo, opening up like a rose, petal by petal, until she reached the highest note of the scale and held the song in full flower there, stretching it out to me like an invitation. After a moment's hesitation, I accepted, and with that our duet began: she with her gorgeous, sensuous purr and I with my gravelly, sulky timbre. At first my voice sounded more like a villain's growl than the dulcet tones of a romantic hero. But as our reconciliation progressed, I was pumped full of Annika's transformative love, and soon I was singing with the tender caresses and eternal promises of a golden, manly tenor. Effortlessly, I scaled the heights and soared over the orchestral plains alongside her. On this magical morning, the curtains parted to reveal the splendor of Annika's beauty and the stamina of a performance that I never would have imagined myself capable of: I was Ferrando, inhaling the sweet breath of love's refreshment; I was Turiddu, tearing up the sheets with sheer godless lust; I was Calaf, singing of love's triumph at the end of a long sleepless night.

This fantasy lingered in my thoughts as I stared now in disbelief at my merciless Annika—my cold-hearted, faithless Annika! There she was, performing a cruel lover's bluff with a determination that I simply could not accept, simply could not fathom. I pleaded with her to drop her mask and reveal her true tender nature to me. I warmed up my voice in the absence of our song, hoping to reinspire her with the impassioned pleas of my solo. When my attempts to soften her failed, I turned to the dark side and tried to force a confession from her: I was Iago, the instigator of tragedy; I was Scarpia, the administrator of threats; I was Pagliaccio, the cuckolded clown howling out his rage and pain before breaking down in a fit of sobbing.

Unmoved, Annika shook her head at me in feigned wonder before resuming her search for her sleep mask. Seeing that my antics were pointless, I collected the remains of my dignity and left the boudoir. I crawled onto the couch and slept until one in the afternoon. Upon waking, I found Malvolio snoozing peacefully by my ear, his breath smelling faintly of booze. I had a massive hangover and my hand was throbbing all over with sharp pains, as if it had been stretched out on a grill and set on fire overnight. With great effort, I trudged into the kitchen where I filled a large stock pot with cold water and a tray of ice cubes. I plunged my hand into the freezing bath and felt immediate relief. But when I pulled it out twenty minutes later, it had turned bright purple and ballooned in size. My stomach lurched and I was hit with an enormous wave of nausea. Like some creature in a B-grade horror film, I staggered into the breakfast nook where Annika was calmly eating half a grapefruit and perusing the Sunday reviews, as if nothing was out of sorts and we had never quarreled.

"Been practicing hard, darling?" she asked, glancing at the swollen mitt that I was brandishing before my chest like a grotesque trophy.

"Better call an ambulance, darling," I said, and fainted dead away from shock.

When I came to, I was lying on an examination table, my hand and forearm bandaged in a puffy, oblong splint that resembled a medical boxing glove. A heavy numbness from my shoulder down told me that a shot of anesthesia had been administered during my hour of unconsciousness. The doctor was a thoroughly unsympathetic soul who kept clicking his ballpoint pen open, closed, open, closed, open, as he gave me the prognosis: I was suffering from an acute case of tendonitis triggered by overuse and would have to lay off the arpeggione for at least twelve weeks, if I wished to see normal function restored to my left hand. My head reeled. Needless to say, a concert performing career was out of the question at this point, as was a recording contract with any half-serious commercial label. At best, with a diligent program of physical therapy, I might hope to regain sufficient motor control to record remedial instruction tapes for beginning music students and weekend hobbyists. However—and here the specialist hit the pause button on his dictation wand and lowered his voice in a semblance of avuncular kindness—he had treated many unfortunate musicians like myself who, when faced with a debilitating injury of this nature, had salvaged their careers by switching to a less demanding instrument, such as the theremin or glass harmonica. With that, the good physician shut his folder and passed me off to his student assistant. After reminding me to get my cortisone prescription filled right away, she urged me to volunteer for a research study led by the physician himself, the results of which would be published in a high-profile medical quarterly. "You really should consider it," I heard her call to my back as I exited. "Your case is a fascinating one. You might even be asked to exhibit yourself at one of our conferences!"

The weeks that followed were bleak and demoralizing. Winter arrived, plunging the city into a deadening gray chill. As my fortunes plummeted, Annika's career took off. Her schedule was busier than ever, with transcontinental invitations scattered in the post for her like confetti. As her absences grew more and more frequent, our relationship continued to deteriorate. I avoided socializing with our friends and soon stopped going out altogether. My one consolation was the weekly shipment containing my orders of rare books and folk music recordings from the farthest reaches of the globe. It was during this wretched period of my existence that I systematically renounced the Western tradition altogether: Bach, Brahms, Bruckner, be gone! Mendelssohn, Mozart, Mussorgsky, into the garbage! Chopin, Schoenberg, Schumann, throw 'em to the dogs! With a bitter heart, I cursed the altar of classical music upon which I had sacrificed and ruined myself. Now I was all about the pentatonic scale, cyclic rhythms, gamelan, and Qawwali. Under the spell of these fascinating, mind-altering sounds, I vowed to abandon my cares and remake myself completely. In the manner of a holy mendicant, I shaved my head, simplified my diet, and took to going barefoot whenever possible. The soles of my feet thickened over time, and soon I was able to negotiate sidewalks and subway platforms with apparent ease. Inspired by the raw textures that unfolded beneath me and the mystical ecstasy revealed to me continuously through my headphones, I learned to move with greater appreciation and accept the conditions of life that had been given to me. After several weeks of concentration and discipline, I no longer flinched at the sight of my crippled hand.

One morning, as I was sitting mindfully on a rattan mat with my eyes closed, Annika arrived home from an overnight flight with her retinue of suitcases and quietly asked me if I had joined a cult. I switched off my music player and asked how her gala concert had gone over in San Francisco.

"Fine," she replied, sinking into an armchair. "Fantastic, in fact. Only . . ."

"What is it?" I asked.

"Well, Beatriz was there," she said. This, I guessed, was Beatriz Garcia-Lopez, Annika's current archrival. An intense young soprano, Beatriz had crafted her voice into a formidable instrument capable of taking on serious bel canto, lyrical spinto, and even dramatic roles.

"I had no idea she was even in the lineup," Annika continued. "Apparently someone dialed her in as a last-minute substitution."

"Let me guess, you got roped into an encore war," I said, repositioning myself on the mat.

"It started out harmless enough," Annika said, "with the usual Mozart and Rossini numbers. You know, a little *Cosi fan tutte*, a little *Barber of Seville*. Richard was there and the three of us did the trio from act 1 of *Cosi*. I delivered an excellent 'Come scoglio,' Beatriz followed with a tolerable 'Una voce poco fa,' and I countered with 'Deh vieni non tardar.' Richard did double duty by us as Figaro."

"Lucky guy," I said, turning my head to the side to stretch my neck.

"I thought that was going to be the end of it, as we took our bows and walked offstage. But no, the applause just kept going until we returned for a second set of bows and walked off again. But those crazy San Franciscans would have none of it. The clapping continued at full blast, and it didn't die down until we came on again and the conductor motioned the orchestra to attention. Well, after that it turned into a kind of free-for-all." She kicked off her heels and sighed.

"What do you mean?" I asked.

"It was down to just Beatriz and me. Richard retreated backstage to rest his voice, and everybody else could tell by the patterns of applause that they weren't wanted."

"I see," I said, a little annoyed by her story so far. "So you had no choice but to engage in a battle of the divas. A duel unto death. First one to cash in her chips bites the dust."

"The atmosphere in the house was positively electric," Annika continued. "Every seat in the War Memorial was filled and some people were still standing from the last ovation. I saw a few of the string players popping uppers, getting ready for the long haul, I suppose."

"Stimulants can be helpful at times," I mumbled.

"And so we were off, trading arias back and forth," Annika said. "Beatriz began with 'Smanie implacabili.' I went in strong with 'O mio bambino caro.' She did Norma's 'Casta diva.' I carried off Amina's sleepwalking number. Then there were the mad scenes—Imogene, Lucia, Elvira. Perhaps it was the influence of the crowd or the stiff competition between us, but we poured ourselves into these roles with new abandon. I have to admit, I was impressed by Beatriz's acting skills, the way she managed to hang on to her high E's without compromising the expressiveness of her face, which looked positively lovesick and deranged. Though with the way she twists her mouth, she's going to have one hell of a mug shot when she retires."

"I saw her portrait in last month's issue of the *Imperator*," I said. "She's already beginning to show her age."

"I'm not surprised, considering how she drinks!" Annika said. "If only her voice would obey the same precipitous decline." She laughed ruefully and extracted a cigarette from her purse.

"Annika, I want you to listen to something . . . but I suppose you'll want to finish your story first," I said. Seeing her cigarette held out expectantly, I dutifully lit it before returning to the mat.

"Oh yes, the encores," she said, after inhaling slowly and deeply. "They seemed to go on for hours, much longer than the concert itself. I was in top form, a little tired at moments, but my voice was in excellent shape and the applause was simply deafening. There was no way that I was going to pass up this chance to take San Francisco by storm. But there was Beatriz. She was not one to be intimidated. Onstage, we were all poise and graciousness—we had enough goodwill between us to pull off the Flower Duet from *Lakme*, for god's sake—but inside us the contest was raging and neither one of us was backing down. Sometimes the applause was louder for me, sometimes for Beatriz. The cheering seemed to ripple across the hall in surges and waves. Over time, it became clear that there were competing factions in the audience. My supporters were in the box seats and first tier, while Beatriz's fans were in the rear orchestra and balconies. As the contest continued, members of our rival teams swept into the aisles, calling out requests and rallying others in the audience wherever they went. They were in a feverish mood, working their way up to a big showdown in the dress circle."

"Did they do it?"

"Oh yes, eventually. But I'm getting ahead of myself. It was all building up to that point—the cycles of fervor and suspense, the cheering and thumping, the torpedoes of bouquets aimed at the stage, the absolute hush that dropped like a blanket over the house whenever one of us stepped forward to begin a new song. When I was singing, all I could hear between the measures was silence—that inhuman silence, the silence of eternity. I often think I must have married that silence before I was born, in some past life perhaps. It's my one passion, the meaning of my existence. My singing is an attempt to move it and change it, make it turn around and speak to me. My fans mean the world to me and I've dedicated my career to them, but I'd give it all up for a single moment alone with that silence, a single moment of recognition."

She paused, gazing intently into the distance. I rested my palms on the mat, afraid to move or speak. She seemed to be making an important confession, a confession that had the power to clarify or break her. She had never looked more beautiful or remote to me. And I knew then that she was lost to me forever, that she had never been mine to begin with. She pulled out of her trance with a shudder. And when she spoke again, her voice had a jaded ring to it. "But all of that is impossible," she said. Suddenly aware of the cigarette stub burning away between her fingers, she put it out in a pot of calla lilies. "Impossible," she repeated, with renewed determination. "Though it does explain why I'd do anything for this. There is very little in this world that matters to me." She turned to me. "Tell me," she said with a note of urgency, "is it wrong to have ambition?"

I stared at her blankly, unsure of what she wanted me to say. She sighed before continuing. "There are many singers in the world, but only a few of us will be remembered and loved when it's all over. If I can't make the silence speak to me, then at least I can win over my listeners and get them to believe I have. And perhaps this belief will be enough to make it all come true."

She shook her head and laughed. "I'm not making much sense, am I? I guess what I'm saying is that I've worked too long and too hard to watch it all come crashing down like this. I want my rightful share. Is that so wrong?"

I thought for a moment before speaking carefully. "You want your rightful share, but there's someone else who wants more than her fair share."

"She's a greedy one," Annika said. "She's a selfish and greedy one, and she doesn't know when it's time to stop. It wouldn't be so bad if she got by on bare talent and craft. That would be halfway respectable. But she insists on being a scene-stealer. She swears by pyrotechnics and razzle-dazzle, and her fans—those poor fools who don't know any better—are totally taken in by the show. They're totally entranced. If only she would stay within the bounds of her training and be a specialist like the rest of us. Instead, she wants to do it all—comedy and tragedy, lyric and dramatic, soubrette and spinto, light opera and grand opera. Next thing you know, she'll be eating like a sumo wrestler and calling herself a Wagnerian. It's perfectly appalling."

"Surely you were able to hold your own with her," I prompted.

"For a while, yes. But then the most horrible thing happened. I started running out of arias. Sure, there were a few melodies I knew by heart, but I hadn't memorized the words yet. And since I couldn't very well scat my way through the murky parts or improvise a new libretto on the spot, I had to stop."

"You stopped singing? Without leaving the stage?"

"It wasn't as bad as it sounds. You see, by that time our fans had collided in the dress circle. And in the tussle that resulted, my team was winning. I had some fierce players, and it gave me great satisfaction to watch them subdue Beatriz's fan base and keep the timid ushers at bay. Her people were all so emotional and overwrought. As soon as she brought out the opening notes of 'La mamma morta,' the swooning began. It was highly irritating and overdone. At the end of the song, the whole symphony lifted itself up like a cape and I heard the pulse of a tambourine. I couldn't believe it—she was making an attempt at Carmen's Habanera! At that point, all hell broke loose. Beatriz's fans were deep in the throes of operatic ecstasy—eyes wide open and fixed, hands held to their breasts, silently protesting that they were but mere mortals, unworthy of such heavenly sounds. As she approached the climax of the piece, an older man, tanned and quite handsome, climbed up on the banister overlooking the orchestra seats and shouted: 'Take me, Beatriz!' He looked as if he was going to do a belly flop into the upstretched arms of the uh, dodge pit . . . squash pit?"

"Mosh pit," I said.

"Yes, that's it. Incredibly, about a minute later, a young man wearing a tattered coat climbed up and did exactly the same thing. After that, the excitement subsided somewhat, which was probably a good thing since the police had arrived, bursting through the doors of the balcony to restrain the two men. They did, however, have enough respect for the arts to wait until the end of Beatriz's final aria before hauling anyone away. Such was the strange scene we found ourselves in at the end of the evening: police in light riot gear, patrons restrained in the aisles, and an entire opera house captivated, held hostage in suspense as Beatriz cleared her throat and the conductor cued the orchestra to play the nostalgic first bars of 'Donde lieta.'"

"Mimi's farewell song?"

"No other, I'm afraid," Annika said. "I didn't think she'd be able to pull it off. With all of her theatrics, I thought, how could she inhabit the soul of this delicate creature and do her any justice? But I was wrong. She sang Mimi beautifully." Annika took out another cigarette with shaking hands. "She sang beautifully," she repeated. "Isn't that the damnedest thing? And everybody knew it. They knew it at once. All her tenderness was concentrated in her voice, and all the world's yearning was fulfilled in that moment when she gathered up her voice and sent it over the heads of the audience to meet the silence at the back of the hall, to meet it with the utmost commitment." She paused, holding out the cigarette for me to light it.

"Her voice had changed and matured in remarkable ways," she continued. "She could do things with it that I could only dream of. When she finished, the whole house basked in the after-tones of her closing notes before breaking into stunned applause. Even the police were clapping. And I was right there with them, in spite of our rivalry, in spite of the understanding that I was raising the white flag. I, Annika Segerstrom, was humbled and defeated. I could never go that far with my voice, I know that." She inhaled and expelled a stream of sad gray smoke. Then she turned to me and gave me a strange look. "Could I?"

I looked away, not knowing how to answer her. In her eyes, I had seen fear, wounded pride, a desire for the impossible that challenged the confines of the truth. She was looking to be rescued by a god or a devil, I didn't know which. Or rather, I did know. She wanted to push her artistry to the highest level, but we both knew that she had a small, fine voice suitable for classical or romantic cadences backed by an orchestra of grace and restraint. It was hardly robust enough to withstand the tempests of the so-called realist school. Only a monster would have encouraged her hopes in this direction. Knowing this, why didn't I tell her the truth?

"Of course you can," I said at last, getting up to wrap a chenille blanket around her shivering frame. "But really, why stop with Mimi? You could go so much farther, do so much more with that voice of yours."

"Cio-Cio-San," she whispered longingly.

"My little butterfly," I said, "The tragic exotics are all the rage again. I read the reviews, you know. Audiences are bored with all that old courtly nonsense, all those tragedies of error committed by neurasthenic heroines. They're hungry for the real deal—darker passions, blood and guts, nineteenth-century verismo with a twentieth-century twist . . ."

"Do you really think?" she said, looking up at me, her eyes shining.

"Yes, I'm sure of it," I said, warming to the argument. "Of course, it will mean many more hours, many more sacrifices. You will have to build and build, and balance the great risks with a dose of caution. But just think of what you could achieve. To beat the unbeatable rival, to dream the impossible dream, to reach the unreachable star—that dream is not impossible, that star is not unreachable! Why bow to Beatriz when Annika can reign supreme?"

I found myself gripping her shoulders tightly. Tears glistened in her eyes as she rose from her chair, clearly carried away by my pep talk. I must have felt moved myself, for my heart was pounding rapidly like a taiko or some other drum of war. I took her face between my hands and kissed her forehead, and sent her off straight away to a master voice coach who lived right on the other side of the park.

Within the week, she embarked on a rigorous program of study, waking up every morning at four, practicing her scales and sostenuto. She trained like an Olympic athlete, adding richness to her timbre and building her vocal weight so that she could cut through a fifty-piece orchestra playing at full blast. It was a heroic campaign and the desired results could soon be heard. Annika had transformed herself into an entirely different kind of soprano. Even her physical appearance had changed to match her new persona. Her hair had grown darker and fuller seemingly of its own accord, for she had relinquished her visits to the beauty salon along with other luxuries for the sake of her artistic goals. Dusky shadows appeared beneath her eyes and a pronounced hollowing at the base of her cheekbones intensified her look of dramatic urgency. The opening of the season saw her debut at Covent Garden as Mimi in *La Boheme*, followed by Amina in *La Somnambula*, and then the title role of *Carmen*, all to considerable acclaim. Between performances, she managed to put in enough hours at the studio to record a selection of lieder by Strauss and lend her voice to the part of Leonore in *Fidelio*. Then it was back to the world stage, where she captivated audiences with a succession of career-building suicides. She disemboweled herself as Cio-Cio-San, hurled herself off a parapet as Tosca, and ascended the funeral pyre as Norma. Finally, after months of continuous singing and carnage, she flew home to the New York stage, where she marched straight to the guillotine as Maddalena.

Her voice didn't suffer the consequences of this overwork right away. But when it did, the damage was irreversible. A subtle, strained wobble began to appear at the ends of her long notes, imperceptible to the untrained ear. Like golden strands frayed at the ends, filaments of sound broke off and hung unpleasantly in midair. Soon this frayed quality became more pronounced. Sometimes the bottom of her voice seemed to drop away. At other times the top of her voice threatened to fly out of control. In either case, her vocal cords were about to snap. Eventually, dropped notes and faulty tunings began to creep into her repertoire. In Buenos Aires, on the closing night of *The Daughter of the Regiment*, she was climbing toward a routine high E-flat when the wobble suddenly reasserted itself and left her finale quite flat. In Montreal, during a solo recital, an inexplicable hoarseness attacked her throat and she resorted to fudging a dozen bars of coloratura to finish her performance. But it was in her beloved Stockholm that catastrophe finally struck. There, in a grand opera house packed with an expectant hometown audience, she lost her voice completely right at the fortissimo climax of her aria. She tried twice, unsuccessfully, to redo the passage until the hissing, booing crowd forced her off the stage. An eager young understudy was promptly ushered into her place.

The news of her final ruin reached me some time after the fact. By then, what remained of our relationship had crumbled beneath the weight of our ill-fated, consecutive downfalls. After moving out of Annika's rooms, I skipped town altogether. With duffel and overcoat in hand, I hailed a cab to the airport, where I purchased a one-way coach ticket to Amsterdam using the wad of hundred-dollar bills I'd found in Annika's vanity. For weeks, I hitchhiked from city to city, frittering away my days at sidewalk cafés and holing up by night in dingy hostels. Preferring my own company, I fended off the various exchange students and budget tourists who wished to engage me in pleasant conversation or a friendly game of cards. Every other night, I'd stop in at a local tavern, often a landmark of some architectural or feudal significance, and get seriously hammered. Occasionally, Annika's blue eyes would appear before me—lost and reproachful—and I'd try in vain to blink away the haunting image. My course through Europe was winding and erratic, but it obeyed a vaguely easterly inclination. By the time of Annika's humiliating Stockholm homecoming, I was philosophically reclined in the third-class compartment of a railcar bound for the Caucasus peaks. Herds of deerlike creatures roamed the grassy steppes. And as the sun rose and bathed the earth in a salmon-colored glow, I could practically hear the strains of a cinematic soundtrack full of desire and damnation, not unlike the prelude from *La Cavilaria Rusticana*. When at last I turned away from the window, it was simply to rest my eyes and whistle a plaintive melody, the refrain of a sinner who had gone too far yet still hoped, in his heart of hearts, to be saved.

The locomotive deposited me at a provincial depot swarming with petty bureaucrats biding their time and grim-faced old women hawking homemade concessions. I bought a hard and tasteless biscuit and settled myself on a large rock on the opposite side of the tracks, some distance away from the unpleasant crowd. Gnawing at the biscuit, I took stock of my situation. I was exhausted and hungry. My clothes were damp and rank, and I needed a bath. I had no home, no lover, no career, no prospects to speak of. To top it off, my therapeutic Bavarian drinking sessions had left me with an overworked liver and a sizable beer gut. In short, my life was utterly worthless and I had nothing left to lose. In my misery, I threw the last bit of biscuit to the wind. As I watched the train depart from the station, I thought that it was only fitting for me to disappear to the ends of the earth—in a journey of escape that I secretly hoped would be my salvation. It wouldn't take long to gather up the necessary provisions. My duffel bag would have to be replaced with something more compact and portable—an aluminum-framed knapsack, if I could find one. I needed a longer jacket and sturdier boots to stand up to wind, rain, monsoon, and any other weather calamity that might blow my way. There was also a call for portable foodstuffs—nuts, dried meats, and bottled water to fortify me on the road, as well as several liters of vodka to be used for barter when the local currency failed me. And I needed batteries. Lots and lots of spare batteries. With any luck, Annika's vanity funds would sustain me all the way to the heart of Asia, where my future would be determined by the whims of fate.

Before beginning my search for supplies, I needed to find temporary lodgings. After making a few inquiries, I made my way across the train tracks, over a clearing strewn with broken bottles and spent condoms, and into the residential part of town, where I arrived at a gray slab of an apartment complex. The building, originally erected as low-cost housing for the early pioneers who had toiled at one of the giant manufacturing plants that loomed nearby, was largely deserted. After the collapse of collectivized industries, it had been taken over by a loose coalition of expatriate squatters, minor criminals, and failed artists. This was the address recommended to me by Bryce Connolly, my erstwhile arranging partner, as a place to collect my thoughts and spend a few nights free of charge.

I was welcomed into the fold by a fellow artist, an agoraphobic oboist who had quit performing publicly and heard about the sudden halt to my own musical career as a manner of introduction from Bryce. After accepting my crippled hand as proof, he motioned me to an unoccupied room with a lumpy, dusty mattress on the floor and a surprisingly beautiful mural of the cosmos painted on the ceiling by a former resident. Later that day and for several days afterward, I went into town to set the details of my expedition in order. I haggled with merchants, studied maps, and debated the pros and cons of various overland routes that more or less approximated the windings of the old Silk Road. In the evenings, I would share a simple repast with the other residents. After dinner, we would sit in front of the stove fire, sipping cups of diluted tea (beer being too rich for the daily household budget) and swapping boastful tales of a dubious autobiographical nature. Every so often, one of us would rise, scavenge the immediate environment for something combustible—a twig, leaf, vegetable stalk, paper scrap, or gum wrapper—and toss it into the stove with a bored, apathetic gesture. The resulting fire was nothing more than a few tendrils of lingering smoke, yet it drew us nightly. Although spring had arrived, the winter frost remained. As the night wore on, we sat shivering in our seats, the outlandish and oft-repeated anecdotes giving way to a chorus of sighs and grumblings. Invariably, someone would suggest that one of the petty thieves in our company should venture out into the streets and pick the pockets of a young American backpacker, or some other such rube foolish enough to be waiting for a train at this hour, in order to secure funds to replenish our tea. The criminal professionals among us would smirk and shoot knowing glances at one another, but in the end not one of them would budge from his seat. Another serving of watery tea would be poured out, weakly savored and consumed, amid a tableau of resignation. For no matter how tiresome we had become to each other, none of us could think of a better way to pass the time than to look around the circle from one miserable face to the next, complaining joyously and endlessly into the night.

After three nights of this, I finally threw up my hands and offered to fetch the tea leaves myself from the one shop that was still open in town. At this announcement, the fire itself seemed to spark up and the room was instantly reanimated. Everyone jumped up at once to put in requests for additional items—a stick of deodorant, a tube of foot cream, a lady's hairbrush, candy bars, a plug of tobacco, a newspaper, the latest issue of *Grazia* or *The Economist*. A paltry installment of coins was pressed into my palms with the tacit understanding that I would be repaid more fully at some later date, as soon as the collective fortunes of the household improved. With this, the squatters returned to their posts and talked among themselves in a spirited way, excited by the treats that they would soon be receiving. I left the building in a state of mild annoyance, glad to take a break from their company. When I returned laden with goods nearly an hour later, I found half the household clinging to one another in a drunken, maudlin mass, singing obscene verses about the government and weeping nostalgically for the good old days that none of them were old enough to remember. The remaining residents had joined as couples or threesomes and were now sprawled across the creaking threadbare sofa, entwined in debauched escapades that might have intrigued me if the participants had been less physically unattractive. In their eagerness to keep the party going, my hosts downed a jug of rubbing alcohol, along with several bottles of cherry-flavored cough syrup. The vile substances were consumed without complaint—malnourishment, hyperglycemia, and unstable brain chemistry facilitating the descent into group hysteria.

At last my preparations were complete. With my knapsack packed and my jacket buttoned up to my chin, I stepped into the chill, crisp dawn and trudged off toward the eastern frontier. My adventures began on an encouraging note. Traveling by foot, I followed flocks of black-and-white sheep over the rocky slopes and into grazing territory, where sequestered valleys and the occasional barn sheltered me from the weather. Each day, I stopped for a simple yet ceremonious lunch at a pleasant location—a dry grassy hillside overlooking the lush valley or a particularly smooth rock with a concave surface to cradle my aching behind. I saw few people except for the rare herdsman on the distant slopes, a curved staff always in hand. One evening, I reached a low dip in a valley and came upon a group of these men gathered around a roasting pit. I listened in rapture as they chanted the hoarse, haunting folk tunes of their forefathers. As I stepped out of the shadows into the firelight, they invited me to sit on a log nearby and offered me a tinful of something I later learned was blood tea. With their permission, I recorded a dozen of their songs using the portable tape deck I'd smuggled out of the States.

Days and weeks passed in a haze of worn mountain ranges and dusty steppes fixed below a slate horizon. Whenever I happened upon a dirt road pointed in my general direction, I'd hitch a ride on a passing wagon cart to rest my wracked frame. My old way of measuring time by Annika's brimming social calendar had vanished. At home in the elements day and night, I began to notice subtle changes in the season—a warmer morning mist, a lightening of cloud cover—and track the movements of Orion and other celestial bodies as they wheeled across the sky.

Eventually, my trajectory brought me to the shore of a green ocean and I prepared to cross what I believed to be the Caspian Sea. Unwilling to part with what little funds I had, I set off upon a barge cobbled together from German automobile tires and equipment parts salvaged from the Soviet-Afghan war. Upon landing ashore, I was promptly abducted by a gang of student radicals and held hostage for eight days, though I was blissfully ignorant of the fact at the time. During my captivity, I remained under the impression that their van was a makeshift hotel shuttle, their ramshackle apartment a low-budget pension, and their crude weaponry and rhetoric an attempt at providing security-conscious hospitality with a touch of local color. They finally released me after discovering that I wasn't the prominent Australian journalist on their watch list and that my audiocassettes contained nothing in the way of inflammatory media, aside from a few herding tunes—denounced as "tourist-trap fakes" by one of my captors, a jaded ex-postdoctoral anthropologist—and an embarrassing poetic monologue full of rage and remorse that I had spontaneously composed months earlier.

A free agent once again, I resumed my overland journey through tense, watchful cities and remote villages that kept time to the rhythms of ancient looms. Along the way, I fed my tape deck a steady stream of batteries and recorded everything of interest that I happened to overhear. I collected bell chimes, prayer chants, hummings, whistled melodies, snatches of song, and loose jam sessions performed on intricate stringed instruments with more intervals, modal scales, and resonances than could possibly be fathomed by my little mind. I was living in a realm of pure sensation, absorbing the sounds around me with minimal assumption and judgment, flooded by their exotic vibrations, accents, and nuances.

As the air got warmer and the land more fertile, the rooftops smoothed into rounded domes and then sharpened into twisty javelin points that pierced the sweltering blue sky. Now more than ever, I kept an eye out for treatable water sources—a tap, well, or clear-running stream—to replenish my battered plastic bottles and stave off dehydration. In the flush of heat, I found my senses growing more and more distorted until my eyes and ears misled me, and I grew fearful of losing my sanity altogether. It was as if the very contours of my self were contracting before being sucked down the tube of a telescope pointing doggedly in the wrong direction: I had succumbed to the inverted gaze of the Orient.

Resting by the side of a dirt road one market day, I ate the leftovers from the previous night's supper, a bun filled with less chicken than cabbage, and grappled with my environment. The cultural and language differences had become insurmountable, my encounters with locals taking on the character of perpetual misunderstanding. A day earlier, I had attempted light pleasant conversation with a young man who furrowed his brows and walked away without a word. Later that same day, hungry and distressed, I had approached an old woman stirring a pot on an open stove. With my eyes most pleading and my hands pressed to my stomach, I spoke the universal language of starvation. She stared at me perplexed, pausing with her spoon in midair, before letting out peals of uncontrollable laughter. Similarly, the locals' words of welcome repelled me and their expressions of outrage amused me. We neatly canceled each other out, but as the interloper, I was the one obliterated by this operation. I wandered the land in a daze, bereft of name and dialect. I shivered in the heat of high noon and perspired at night. Only the mosquitoes were attracted to me, but even they lost interest after a few bites, buzzing off before too long in dizzying circles.

The one thing that sustained me during this difficult stage of my travels was the promise of obtaining rare and valuable new field recordings. I would follow groups of spectators into teahouses and wedding halls, where singing contests and instrumental ensembles were under way. Sneaking up to the front row and crouching down to make myself as inconspicuous as possible, I would point my microphone, concealed by a handkerchief, toward the stage and depress the record button.

In this furtive manner, I greedily filled up cassette after cassette, believing it was only a matter of time before my foreignness would be noticed and get me booted out. But the audience never seemed to pay me any mind, so captivated were they by the sounds they had come to hear.

Over time, I developed a knack for finding the best venues in which to loiter and drink indefinitely, in the hopes of catching an impromptu performance. Often stationed in an undersized folding chair in front of a small round table, I made a habit of scanning the crowd for the faces that had become familiar to me— these were the diehard aficionados, many of them accomplished artists in their own right, who followed the finest vocalists and musicians from village to village. I watched with longing as these men greeted each other with winks and nudges, tapping their feet deftly to the polyrhythms, leaning in from time to time to comment on a striking passage of melody or improvisation. Sometimes one or more of them would be invited to join the ensemble onstage for a few numbers. On these occasions, the others would sit back and listen appreciatively, their animated faces exuding a fraternal spirit of camaraderie and mischief.

One evening, during an irksome session in which I kept struggling with a tape cassette that threatened to unravel, I felt the sudden presence of someone at my side. It was one of the fraternity boys, a young fellow with a thick thatch of hair, who slipped noiselessly into a seat at my table and set down a plate of fried dough balls. He tapped the edge of the plate in a friendly and persistent manner until I helped myself to a snack. After I finished half of a doughnut with a gratified look, we turned back to the show, a bit of puppetry accompanied by a band of reeds and double-headed drums. Over the course of the performance, other members straggled in one by one, carrying casks of wine and settling casually around us. By the end of the evening, I found myself surrounded by the men whom I had watched on countless occasions, a confirmed pledge to their brotherhood.

As they made me feel at home in their company, the great weight of my loneliness began to lift.

During the performances, I kept myself attuned to bits and pieces in the crosstalk that I was beginning to understand. I watched looks and gestures more closely, using them as guides to my word discoveries. I would try out a word or phrase on the brothers, delighted when they nodded excitedly and spoke to me as if I was no longer the awkward foreigner among them. One morning, the same young fellow who originally approached me insisted that I attend his sister's wedding later that afternoon. I watched the ceremony with interest and then followed the others to a nearby reception hall where the party was already under way. The chords coming from the hall were different from what I had encountered so far, yet strangely familiar. As I entered, I was taken aback by the scene before me. The young fellow was onstage strumming the guitar and belting out the lyrics to "In My Life" by the Beatles. His English pronunciation was imperfect with a faintly British intonation, suggesting some time spent in school or the lucrative alleyways of the tourist district. As he concluded his performance, other members of the fraternity gathered around my astonished figure, their faces alight and their bodies doubling over with laughter. They swept me up onto the stage, where I was persuaded to join the company in several enthusiastic, drunken choruses of "Rocky Raccoon."

My new friends taught me how to hear with an expanded ear, an ear that listened not only for local innovations in rhythm and pitch, but also for the so-called "music of the spheres"—the vast, transpersonal echo emanating from the core of the composition, sweeping backward and forward across time and human history. They conducted themselves with rough elegance, exhibiting an urbane sensibility that seemed to belie their provincial origins. To my relief, they voiced no objections to my recording project and even encouraged my efforts, supplying me with fresh batteries whenever I ran low and making opinionated, at times contentious, recommendations as to which artists I should pursue next.

One name that came up again and again was that of a legendary conductor who had achieved unprecedented fame on the national level, dominating all the choice venues, making headlines in the media, and becoming a recognized authority on music and the arts in general, only to retire abruptly at the age of thirty-nine at the peak of his career. During his professional years, he had been known as an avowed traditionalist, driving his ensembles to note-by-note executions of classical compositions and ever higher standards of perfection. Now, some said, he had retreated to the countryside to live a life of seclusion and contemplation: meditating, praying, reading, teaching occasionally, and performing once a year in secret for a select group of friends, students, and admirers. Others denied these accounts and claimed that he had turned his energies to composition, creating a body of original work that incorporated classical forms yet transformed them in radical ways—layering the new over the old, or the old over the new—resulting in textures of sound that defied technical description and appealed directly to the emotions. Still others questioned his very role as a conductor, casting him instead as an anti-conductor who experimented with the very notion of ensemble itself. In these versions, he interjected no directive or will of his own other than to facilitate the improvisations of his musicians. The resulting musical lines, lightly cued and shaped by his ear, intermixed to make a daring polyphony of collective invention.

As the story shifted or changed entirely from one adamant narrator to another, it became impossible to know which version was closest to the truth. Everyone wanted me to believe his particular account, throwing up his hands in frustration when I stared at him uncertainly. One day, I was introduced to a clairvoyant old woman who provided yet another variant of the narrative. She was the grandmother of the young fellow who spoke some English, and he served as our interpreter. According to her, the legendary conductor now spent his days and nights hiking through the forest with a notebook in hand. (She paused to pick up a stick and drew a large rectangle in the dirt.) She described how he filled its pages with intricate notations depicting the sounds of the rustling trees, chirping birds, buzzing insects, and flowing river water, the miracles of life brought forth from the four thousand and ninety-six varieties of sunlight. (She motioned the stick in an upward arc across the sky.) Once he finished his notes, he would bring the pages back to his studio where gifted students would be waiting. Together they would sight-read the score, inserting no downbeats or notes of emphasis, entrusting themselves fully to the workings of nature. His goal was to rehearse his musicians steadily toward the crowning act of devotion: a twenty-four-hour performance in which they would reproduce, tone by tone, the unfolding of an entire day. The symphony would take place in the open air, where the music would intermingle with live sounds. Meanwhile, the audience would be encouraged to come and go as they pleased, so that they might experience time moving forward in step with its representation. It would be through this performance that the legendary conductor—no longer a mere traditionalist or one of the avant-garde—would adhere to the vision of the most ancient and wondrous composer of all.

In the final chapter of this ever-changing story told to me over several weeks, the conductor was reputed to have turned away an envoy of the court dispatched to award him a royal honor. He had also thwarted the aims of countless journalists, biographers, and scholars who had journeyed from afar in search of him. Despite his antisocial personality, the barriers I faced culturally as an outsider, and my resistance to renew my travels, it was decided by popular vote that I should seek out this renowned recluse at once, in the hopes of making an exclusive recording that might be made available to the national listening public and beyond. To this end, the brotherhood composed a long letter of introduction, which they handed off to an associate whom they believed would know how to begin routing it to its addressee. Over the next several days, they supplied me with maps depicting various approaches to several villages where the conductor might be sequestered. At the farewell party, they toasted me with overconfident cheers and drank heartily to my health.

Thus began my ill-starred journey to the interior. I slogged along the riverbank in a southwesterly direction until I came across a tributary where a great banyan tree had taken root. After admiring its many trunks, I turned left and followed the waterway as instructed until I reached the first of the villages. Hungry and weary from my travels, I stopped at the one guesthouse in town and enjoyed an excellent meal. However, after engaging a few memorable characters there in conversation, I discovered no trace of the conductor. Nor did I fare any better at the next village or the one after that. Expecting nothing more, I felt little disappointment. I was relishing the opportunity to collect authentic examples of the local music, even if I was unable to find the celebrity in question.

As I continued my journey to each of the villages circled on the map, I found myself looking out on terraced crops plowed by water oxen. My simple lunches of sticky rice wrapped in banana leaves took on a romantic flavor, as I pictured myself the wayward hero of a harrowing tale. Images of reality, however, soon intruded on my reverie. I began to notice the spread of Western pop culture and learned that recent infrastructural projects had included the installation of a satellite dish network in the region. This pernicious colonization manifested itself in the form of television sets, botched Hollywood lingo, and teenagers dressed in T-shirts printed with slogans of the toxic Me generation. But worst of all were the radio programs, broadcast over airwaves of international tastelessness, spewing the cheesiest and most square-sounding remixes of American Billboard hits onto the developing world.

One day, as I languished in the humidity of a small restaurant specializing in fried dumplings and home-brew, my ears were assaulted by a terrible noise sputtering out from the speakers above the entrance to the kitchen. I snatched up my knapsack, determined to escape the Muzak as soon as possible, but something about the tune sounded uncannily familiar and I dropped back in my seat, transfixed. I listened with growing comprehension and horror. There was no doubt about it; the flourishes and instrumentation were unmistakable. It was none other than my own easy-listening version of "Surf's Up"—the last score I had been working on with my former arranging partner, Bryce Connolly. This unexpected collision with my past sent me into a tailspin. I flagged down the young waitress on duty and ordered a bottle of beer. And another and another. I could barely make sense of my hopelessness. Perhaps it was the tragedy of seeing a sensitive culture infiltrated by the crassness of global consumerism and witnessing my own role in this corruption. Perhaps it was the mere awfulness of the arrangement itself, the fact that I was largely to blame for its existence. Was this how I would be remembered: as a creator of meaningless kitsch, someone who had turned a pop masterpiece into an annoyance, an insufferable piece of fluff? Or perhaps it was the sting of Bryce's betrayal, the fact that he had capitalized on our collaboration without my knowledge and was no doubt growing rich on the royalties. In any case, I drank to forget my humiliation and then I drank some more to drown my despair. At beer number four, I became fast friends with the farmers sitting at the next table and showered them with rounds of drinks. At number seven, I became excessively jolly. There were hoots and hollers, possibly some kind of dancing, a swirl of colors spinning round and round in time with my thoughts. At number ten or eleven, the world came swinging at me like a giant fist and I swung back. At number thirteen, darkness descended and I was relieved of consciousness altogether.

When I came to, I was lying on a short, cotton mattress beneath a sea-green quilt and a pile of ropy weights, which turned out to be my own arms and legs leaden with the aftereffects of heavy intoxication. Strong yeasty smells and an assortment of hanging pans told me that I was in a kitchen. Rolling over with some effort, I looked toward a large window and absorbed the soft golden light streaming into the room—such a calm and peaceful light, suffused with blossoms and birdsong and the ripening heat of afternoon. I would have been happy to bask in it for days on end, losing myself in the sweet oblivion of its warmth, had it not been for the sudden appearance of a tiny middle-aged woman. Taking no notice of me, she stationed herself by the window sill and began cheerfully tossing the contents of my knapsack, one by one, out through the opening. Numb and strangely detached, I watched as she fished out cassette after cassette filled with priceless field recordings, pausing a moment to examine the handwriting scribbled on each one before launching it into flight with a deft flick of her miniature wrist. And that was when I heard an entirely new kind of music—the poignant whistling of my possessions as they went sailing through the window on their way to the resident garbage heap, which received them all with a resonant squelch. (To this day, I cannot hear a squelch, or the sound of any object hitting and sinking into a moist surface, without tears welling up in my eyes.) My hostess worked with remarkable speed and vigor, her eyes sparkling as she lightened my load. Coming across my boxer shorts and socks, she shook them out of the bag and deposited them in a basket. When she got to my recording machine, she held it up with solemn care and set it aside.

At last she finished her work and turned toward me. Upon seeing that I was awake, she broke into a wide toothy grin and hurried over to excavate me from my torpor. Before I knew what was happening, she pulled the pillow out from under my head and propped it up against the wall. When it slid back down, she hit it a few times with the palm of her hand until it succumbed to her. I promptly pulled myself up to a sitting position. Satisfied, she turned away to the stove and returned with a bowl of noodles in a rich broth. I finished eating, appreciating the soul food after my night of imbibing liquid poison, and closed my eyes to assess my massive hangover. Before I could determine if I was hearing pounding hammers or approaching footsteps, I felt a viselike grip on my funny bone. Although she had the stature of a munchkin and I resisted her with all my might, my hostess managed to drag me off the mattress and over to a large round table. I plopped down on a low stool, my head spinning from the sudden movements. On the table, there were stacks of thin pancakelike discs and a tremendous vat of savory filling. By this time, I had acquired the rudiments of the national tongue but the woman spoke only a downriver dialect, so that our communications were conducted largely in pantomime. I watched her snatch up a fresh dumpling wrapper, scoop a spoonful of filling into its center, crimp to seal its moistened edges, and wait for me to do the same. It was then that I realized the reason for her maddening cheerfulness—my labor would be required in exchange for her overnight lodgings and amenities.

And so I remained there, in that infernal kitchen, as her captive. I don't know how I managed to cope or how long my captivity lasted. Time passed. The sun got hotter and hotter, stretching the sky out like a balloon until a piece of it popped open and dumped torrents of rain onto the village—onto its unpaved roads, its squares of thirsty crops, and its population of long-suffering inhabitants who hurried back to their huts to escape the storm. Only the children made the most of the moment, running down to the river and wading across the muddy waters with great animal splashes, getting joyously drenched to the bone. When the rains stopped, a stillness descended and the season cooled down by a few blessed degrees. Customers came and went, demanding plates of dumplings and bottles of beer. I took on various responsibilities—fetching ice, bussing tables, stirring the tubs of slowly fermenting brew in the dirt yard—but mostly I was stationed at the table in the kitchen where I was seldom alone. My fellow dumpling folders were mainly children between the ages of six and twenty. Contrary to my initial assumptions, I had not stumbled onto a den of child labor. It was difficult to determine which of the children were related by blood to the proprietress, or which had simply come over to play and felt obligated to show deference to her as their elder by folding a few dumplings before returning home. In either case, they were free to come and go as they pleased. But when the restaurant was particularly busy and orders were piling up fast, a stern look from the proprietress was enough to freeze them into place as obedient volunteers. When I saw the precision of their handiwork, I devoted myself wholeheartedly to the improvement of my folding technique. After some time, my dumplings became less misshapen, and I no longer suffered the slings and arrows of the children's ridicule.

The only one who ever gave the proprietress any back talk was the young waitress, who was a character in her own right. Her lines, from what I could make of them, were so sassy and outlandish that the proprietress—her mother or aunt, I thought—could only reel back in mock horror before bursting into laughter. As the restaurant's sole waitress, she had become a sort of entertainment center, kidding the regulars mercilessly and keeping the more unruly patrons in check. She was fluent in at least five different dialects especially with regard to swear words, which she patiently taught to her younger siblings or cousins until they too learned how to cuss like pirates. Aside from her calling out colorful directions when I gave her occasional rides to town on the delivery scooter, I had exchanged only a few words with her. One day, when we were ladling fresh beer into bottles, I muttered a question to myself about the fermentation process and jumped up when she delivered a detailed scientific explanation in flawless Midwestern English. As I picked up the bottles I'd knocked over, she explained that she was a junior at the University of Illinois at Urbana-Champaign, double-majoring in biology and philosophy, and was taking a year off to help her aunt and uncle with their restaurant business. When she returned to the States, she planned to continue her schooling and become a medical doctor or liberal arts professor. Intrigued, I found a copy of one of her papers on my stool the next day—a comparative minitreatise on Kierkegaard and Dostoevsky.

I forgot all about the elusive conductor until one evening in the middle of the dry season. It was a fine night with a lively chorus of frogs and cicadas, and a great round moon rising outside the kitchen window. I was stooped over the table, folding and joking with a larger-than-usual contingent of volunteers, when the notes of a melody came tinkling into the room like a handful of slowly tumbling coins. I stopped what I was doing and sat up at once, listening. The solo was being played sweetly and plaintively on a stringed instrument, and was coming from the woodland between the restaurant and the river. Captivated, I dropped a half-folded dumpling onto the stone floor, its ball of filling rolling out of its wrapper amid a dozen pairs of bare dangling legs. I looked at the others, their hands working busily without any change to their record pace or workmanship. But when the melody rose to its expressive climax and repeated a single plucked note with an almost aching emphasis, the world seemed to hang in midair and everything—the moon, the frogs, the joking talk and fast-moving fingers of the dumpling folders—halted in sublime appreciation.

The music resurfaced over the next six nights, sometimes played solo, sometimes in ensemble, sometimes plucked on strings, sometimes struck on metallic bell-like keys. Although it was often joined by a small corps of hand drums, it always featured the same underlying theme, the same basic melody reinterpreted with infinite variety and range of emotion. One night I heard yearning transforming into pure joy. The next night I heard an opening attack of jealousy followed by pride, uncertainty, and regret in rapid succession. The night after that I heard sadness plunging to despair, then slowly lifting until it came to rest at a place I could only describe as nonyearning. Finally, the theme was reprised again with a long string solo that started out slow, threading its way through a few tender notes of the scale, then gradually mounting in tempo and complexity to weave a fabric of sound larger than any single player or ensemble, larger than humanity itself. When the performance ended, I found myself staring out at the edge of the black forest through the kitchen window, my mouth agape in awe and wonder.

After seven consecutive nights, the music suddenly stopped and was replaced by silence. In each of its variations, I had felt certain that I was hearing the guiding hand of the legendary conductor. In the daytime, I tramped back and forth through the woods, combing every inch of ground where the musicians must have been stationed, but the only thing I ever found was a small dulcimer mallet.

Still, this object was tangible evidence and it gave me the assurance I needed to not ignore what had transpired before me. I knew better than to bring up the topic with the proprietress, so I approached the young waitress who had become by now if not quite a friend, then a sort of younger sister whom I could count on to half-amuse and half-irk me on a daily basis. But when I mentioned the mysterious nocturnal music to her, she only shook her head without answering any of my questions. Later that day, I spotted her talking with the proprietress in the pantry and slipped behind a carved screen to observe them unseen. Although they were too far away for me to make out what they were saying, the confidential tilt of their heads and their hushed manner indicated that they were discussing the matter at hand. Near the end of their tête-à-tête, the proprietress appeared to be struck by an idea and they nodded to each other conspiratorially before being overtaken by the giggles like a couple of schoolgirls. After a few minutes of this, the proprietress waved a hand, commanding silence from them both, and they marched past my hiding place, retying their apron strings as they headed out of the kitchen.

Two, maybe three weeks passed with dull regularity. I heard no more music in the night and nothing more was said on the matter. Then one morning at dawn, as I lay on my mattress in the kitchen slumbering peacefully, I was shaken awake by a persistent force at my ankle. It was one of the proprietress' nephews, a teenager who was always clowning around and had a birthmark covering the right side of his face. I thought this mark suited him, giving the young man the perpetual look of a harlequin. With bemused gestures, he gave me to understand that I was to get up and follow him out to the woods, where my new morning duties awaited. Still sleepy and feeling like the household minion, I wondered what I would find there—a gigantic tub of brew that required stirring with a long pole from the perch of a treetop? After grumbling about the ungodliness of rising at this hour to the young man's considerable delight, I managed to find my hat and trampled after him.

I followed him past the brew shed, across the dirt yard, and into the same woods I had reconnoitered weeks earlier. When we reached a large tree stump seared by a past fire, the young man turned left and led me down an embankment to a small clearing ringed by saplings. The sun was only just climbing over the rim and the delicate leaves shimmered light pink in the crimson light. Within moments of our arrival, I heard a high-pitched whine. On the other side of the clearing, there was a rain barrel, next to the barrel stood a covered pen, and inside the pen there was an animal. At first I thought it was a fox, its face triangular with short upright ears and a long pointed muzzle, its legs slender and nimble. But when it moved to the side, I saw that it was a size larger, its sandy grey body marked with small black spots and rings on its tail. As the boy swung open the door of the pen to put on its halter and lead, the animal made a few quick turns and eyed me appraisingly.

This half-tame creature, the boy explained, had been raised by his family, less as a pet than as a working member of the community. In the afternoons, she was let loose near the village to keep the rodent population down. But she didn't like to be penned up for long and was anxious to get out each morning at dawn. This chore was normally the boy's, but would now fall upon me instead, what with the school term beginning and his parents insisting that he study more. He spoke the creature's name, a long multisyllabic word that I had no chance of pronouncing properly. The nearest approximation I could manage was "Agatha." And that was how I came to know her, as Agatha. Agatha the dancing beast. The boy talked to her fondly before handing me her lead with a grin and scampering off.

Immediately Agatha began to pull on the lead. She pressed her ears flat against the top of her head and pointed her entire body—from the light-colored tip of her tail to her amber eyes—toward an opening in the brush that was far too small to admit a creature of my size. I tugged on the lead to make her turn around, but she would have none of it. She reared up several times, arching her back and thrashing her tail in the underbrush. Seeing no other way out of my predicament, I slackened my hold, giving her just enough lead to surge forward and bring me to the opening. Getting down on my hands and knees, pushing back branch after branch (their prickly arms snapping back into place and poking at me as soon as I released them), and crawling on my belly like a great lizard, I eventually made it out to the other side. As soon as I finished dusting off, Agatha again pulled on the lead, and this time I gave her free rein. As the woods whisked past me, I realized that I was once again submitting to the will of a creature smaller and more determined than myself. Agatha finally stopped, after having led me through several more fraught passages, and I looked around in disbelief. A radiant shower of sunlight penetrated the dense forest canopy. Thick vines wrapped around the tree trunks and vast fronds reached outward with great leafy fingers. I could hear the joyful trickling of a small stream somewhere beneath the carpet of sedge.

The sudden tightening of the lead brought me back to attention. Agatha had stopped at a ylang-ylang tree with a heady scent that momentarily reminded me of Annika, and was busy circling it. Fast and furious, I disentangled the lead by circling the tree a few times in the opposite direction. Wiping the perspiration from my brow, I spotted a fallen log nearby and tried to persuade Agatha to move toward it, but she would not be budged. I hesitated. Eventually, I drew a deep breath and, praying that I would not be scratched or bitten to death in the process, removed the halter from her body. She trotted over at once to a square of sunlight, crouched down low, and waited. Meanwhile, I sat down on the log and watched her, grateful to rest after the many dips, loops, and dashes I had performed that morning in following her.

We remained in our respective positions with only the trickling of the stream to mark the passage of time. After a while, I heard a light rustling high up in the leaves. Agatha silently rose, gazing up into the canopy of the ylang-ylang expectantly, her tail swishing back and forth. A great feathered bird—about the size of a parrot with a bright blue head and a profusion of green, gold, and red plumage—came swooping down from the branches, making a wide, low-altitude circuit of the copse before shooting back up to its perch like a rocket. It repeated this grand flight pattern two more times. Meanwhile, Agatha followed the bird's movements with her eyes, tensing her haunches and readying herself for the pounce. As the bird came down for a third round,

Agatha lunged after its tail feathers. Although she missed her mark, the force of her momentum carried her up to a low branch of a neighboring tree, where she was well-positioned to continue the chase. Round and round they went, bird and beast in virtual lockstep. Agatha bounded across the sedge, up and down tree trunks, and from branch to branch in swift pursuit. Sometimes she would stop to catch her breath or make a coughing noise after missing a jump. Sometimes the bird would skid to a stop in midflight, squawk uproariously, and reverse its direction, giving chase to Agatha for a change. With the bird on her heels, Agatha would dive into the safety of the tall grasses with her tail tucked between her legs. Once the bird flew away, she would look about timidly, slowly regaining her confidence before picking up the chase again. Finally, the contest seemed to end in a draw. The bird retreated to its elevated perch and Agatha strutted over to the square of sunlight, where she washed her coat regally, careful not to betray the slightest sign of fatigue. When the light drifted, leaving the length of her body in shadow, she rose as if on cue and trotted over toward me to receive her halter.

Over the days that turned into weeks, Agatha and I established a genuine rapport. When I approached her pen each morning at dawn, she would greet me with a laughing noise. Together we would tunnel through the brush to the little ylang-ylang forest, where she and the great feathered bird would engage in their ritual chase. I looked forward to the chase each morning with fresh anticipation. The movements of the animals both excited and calmed me, leaving me with feelings of vitality and peace. After removing Agatha's halter, I liked to lie with my eyes closed on the log, listening intently for the sounds of the forest. At first the woods would be quiet and serene, marked only by buzzing insects and the steady trickling of the stream. I would feel myself become one with these elements, drinking in their familiarity. Then new sounds would vibrate in my ear: the light rustling of leaves followed by several branches clattering against each other in a rapid lead-in rhythm. After a few moments of suspense, I would hear wings flapping against the air, the sound advancing and retreating in cycles. Then the scuffling of paws along the forest floor followed by the distinct sounds of the chase—claws hitting tree bark, twigs snapping, a thud on the ground followed by the subtle vibrations of the earth, a cough, a squawk, silence. And then the sounds would repeat at different pitches and tempos, sometimes softer or louder, sometimes slower or faster. While listening, I would picture Agatha—her intelligent face, her beautiful spotted coat, her nimble legs. And the bird—its proud head, its great kaleidoscopic wings, its artful reversal of the chase. And the ylang-ylang—its central location in the little forest, its white flowers, its familiar scent. And I would sometimes feel tears streaming down my face as I lay there, tears of acceptance, tears of contentment. When Agatha finally trotted toward me, I would put on her halter with feelings of deep affection and admiration.

I can't think of a time when I ever felt happier than in those moments I spent with Agatha in the little forest. Thirsty and sleepy, I liked to rest my hand on the furry warmth of her broadside as she napped in the square of sunlight after the chase, petting her ever so softly, ever so reverently. I wanted to experience the world through her presence, wishing I could know even half of what she knew. And through it all, Agatha would simply close her eyes and nap, absorbing the whole world around her—the sunlight, the tropical heat, the coolness of the sedge—into her body. She was content. She had material belief.

On my way back to the restaurant after exercising Agatha, I would pass through the woodland and recall the seven nights of music that it had mysteriously brought forth. One day, I rested on the seared tree stump there before returning to the kitchen. In my mind's wanderings, I remembered the story of the clairvoyant old woman, her vision of the legendary conductor hiking through the forest, making annotations in his notebook, and composing a score to represent the sounds of the natural world. Picking up a stick, I decided to return to my musical roots and mentally compose my own score for the more salient features of the chase. I began with seven lead-in beats representing the rustling leaves prior to the entrance of the bird. (I rapped the stick seven times against the stump.) Next, there would be a major downbeat signaling the start of the bird's first proud orbital sweep, with eight counts representing each circuit of the copse. (I drew a wide circle in the dirt, with eight notches etched at regular intervals around the dial.) The initial beat of the fourth circuit would signal Agatha's first pounce, closely followed by a timed pattern of pursuit with thirty-two beats depicting her scuffling paws. The resonant notes between the counts would portray the trickling stream. All in all, there would be twenty-four grand cycles of thirty-two counts each, subdivided into eight-beat base cycles with regular syncopation. True to the spirit of the conductor, the performance would take place in the forest where the music had originated. Seized by inspiration, I hopped up onto the stump and imagined myself conducting an orchestra of bells and metallophones, thumping my lead drum with emphasis, shaking my head at an errant player who struck his keys too slowly to represent Agatha's movements with any fidelity. I led the ghost orchestra through four cycles, and then abruptly sat back down and stared at the surrounding woodland in a daze. Could this have been the very spot where the conductor himself had stood weeks earlier?

A few days later, I was approached by the proprietress and her niece, my learned friend Moa, in the kitchen. As I folded a dumpling with factory precision, the proprietress lightly grunted approval and prodded me until I turned around on the stool to face her. Straightening her apron, she indicated that Moa had something to say. After a moment of respectful hesitation in her aunt's presence rewarded by the swat of a dishrag, Moa announced that she was getting ready to return to school and, having racked up enough frequent flier miles to earn a free companion ticket, proposed that I accompany her as far as Los Angeles. After mulling over the decision for a few days, I agreed to go, hoping that the commercial airwaves and palm trees would ease the challenging and no doubt bittersweet matter of my repatriation into ordinary civilian life. By this time, I was being treated all around like family and the question of my captivity, if there ever was such a thing, was a moot one. Two weeks before our scheduled departure, I was officially introduced to the conductor by the beaming proprietress, who seemed to produce him out of thin air, along with my confiscated recording machine and a fresh packet of blank cassettes.

What I mean to say is this. One moment, I was standing next to Moa, discussing the details of that night's bar menu. The next moment, I was shaking hands with a tall, elegantly dressed gentlemen in his early fifties, with silver sideburns and a lively, intelligent look in his eyes. Between these two moments, I lived what? A hypothesis, a hallucination, a dream in the jungle? Episodes from my recent and distant past flashed before my eyes, and I realized with a start that my life was no longer an absurdity. I made my acquaintance with the conductor, who was the proprietress' husband and Moa's uncle. (I half-wondered how I had never stumbled upon him earlier, though I surmised this plan and its careful execution to be the proprietress' handiwork.) He led me to a secluded, though by no means inaccessible, area of the forest where his secret ensemble rehearsed. Together, we made two decent recordings, followed by a third extended session that turned into one of those once-in-a-lifetime recordings, simply unsurpassed in composition and expression. This recording cemented my reputation when I returned to the States and signaled the start of a meaningful, albeit lawless, career.

Why am I telling you this? I doubt that you will be able to understand or even appreciate the subtlety of musical experience I'm speaking of here. Over the centuries, the human ear has evolved from a tuning device to a filtering device. These days, it's all just noise or silence, silence or noise—all you can do is make your choice and live with it. Still, I'm approaching the end of my story and we're drawing near the part that will really matter to you, the part I've been meaning to get to for your sakes. I can't leave you hanging, so let us go back to a certain terminal at LAX where I have just landed, jet-lagged and disoriented from the fourteen-hour flight over the Pacific. After emerging from an accordionlike tunnel with forced air blowing through its vents, Moa and I stopped at an overpriced airport restaurant for a mediocre meal of cocktail nuts, pizza, and soda. We stretched our legs, killed time by concocting tales about the other travelers sprawled around us in the waiting area, and promised to keep in touch. Outside, airplanes kept taking off and landing within view of the big central tower, which looked like a prop from a vintage sci-fi movie, a dream of the future invented by a denizen of the past. We said our farewells, and I watched my friend board and then take off fifteen minutes later on her connecting flight to Chicago.

After Moa's departure, I was left with a powerful feeling of emptiness. In the pocket of my jeans, I had a slip of paper with the numbers of various contacts and leads in Southern California—old classmates from the music conservatory, friends of Moa, friends of Moa's friends, impresarios. But instead of looking for a phone booth, I went straight to the local transportation counter and rented a car, a shiny blue Pontiac convertible with a leather-trimmed steering wheel and AM/FM radio player. For three whole days, all I did was drive with the top down through the streets of West LA, slurping sodas and listening to inane pop music, taking in the sights and sounds of the sunny overbaked landscape, its acres of entertainment and retail spaces a picture postcard of commercial luxury: Santa Monica Boulevard, Barrington Avenue, Sunset Boulevard, Bundy Drive. On the final day, I decided to drive straight down Wilshire Boulevard from end to end and beyond, west to east, beach to barrio. I started out around noon and was soon clocking an easy forty-five miles per hour, counting federal buildings and synagogues and Bob's Big Boys by the minute. As I crossed into the Miracle Mile, my eye was drawn to a handsome wrought-iron fence spanning the greater length of a city block, with a sign of some sort on it. Pulling up, I looked beyond the fence and saw a bizarre-looking swamp, vast pits of bubbling tar surrounded by a well-kept lawn. On the far side of the largest pit, I saw a harrowing sight: a family of elephants in distress, an adult and calf lowing helplessly on the shore as another adult sank down past its knees into the tar, fatally trapped by the quicksand effects of the bitumen. Yet when I looked again, I saw that these weren't modern-day elephants but tusked mastodons, made not of flesh but of painted resin, life-sized sculptures arranged into a tableau of prehistoric woe. At that same moment, a bus coach pulled into the parking lot alongside the fence and deposited a group of tourists onto the sidewalk. Garrulous and garishly dressed, their happy faces in sharp contrast to the tragic scene before them, they filed in through the doors of a nearby building. I followed them, my curiosity piqued.

I found myself standing in the lobby of a museum that must have been designed and built in the 1970s. Plaques and information boards were bolted to bare concrete walls, and a reception kiosk gave entrance to a carpeted exhibition room. I paid the admission fee and followed the tail of the tourist group inside. Members of the group had already fanned out among the interactive stations, pushing red buttons to illuminate different areas of a Pleistocene diorama, tugging in vain at a weighty dumbbell submerged in a bucket of demonstration tar.

I moved past them to a large glass-enclosed terrarium stocked with ancient ferns and palms, and I immediately thought of Agatha, how her ancestors of forty thousand years ago would have felt right at home. Scanning the room, I saw several walls decorated with murals of natural selection in action—herbivores, carnivores, and scavengers locked in the eternal struggle for survival. Another wall was covered with rows of fossilized wolf skulls, a sampling of the life that had perished in the pits. I was drawn to a vertical display case where the likeness of a beautiful longhaired woman stood demurely. Suddenly a curtain of darkness swept through her body, transforming her flesh into a column of human bones. A few seconds later, the skeleton vanished and the woman reappeared. But her beauty was no longer the same and I quickly turned away before the morbid transformation took place again. Ungovernable feelings flowed through my body, and I experienced them all with the aloofness and repose of a temporarily placeless person, a noncitizen of humanity.

Finally, I came to the highlight of my visit: a towering animatronic model of a saber-toothed tiger and a giant sloth. Like the interplay between Agatha and the bird, this contest was officially a duet, though its movements were controlled by a hunk of aging technology, its outcome artificially choreographed. I will leave you here now, standing at the base of the exhibit, your faces upturned and slightly flushed from the radiating spotlight. Imagine the acres of parking lots around you melting, liquefying into primordial asphalt. Street lamps are drowning, the automobile is going extinct. Actually, there's a strange sense of relief, isn't there? A strange, dreamy quality about this bubbling tar, this byproduct of geology that never quite reached the spark and drive of refined petroleum, flammable oil, high-octane fuel. With this crude substance, let us pave the globe—but that will all come in time. For now, continue to wade in this infernal swimming pool. The giant sloth has landed, its hind legs planted in the muck. Poised above it is the saber-toothed tiger, its jaws flexed. But let us experience this properly, from the beginning. The animals are at rest, separated by a distance of a few feet. All is quiet. Then a timer ticks into action, a motor kicks up, and the models begin to slide on their mounts. The big cat lunges with claws outstretched and clamps onto the neck of the sloth, as roars issue from a monospeaker installed near the exhibit sign. The sloth rears up in alarm and raises its left forefoot in a pose of mortal pathos. The long digits of the forefoot, similar to a human hand, are stretched skyward and curled tensely at the tips, calling to mind Picasso's *Guernica* or Rodin's *Burghers of Calais*. The action lasts all of twelve, maybe thirteen seconds. At the end of this time, the cat's fangs are suspended in midair, less than an inch away from the sloth's neck. No blood is drawn, no appetite is sated. The inevitability of nature is stalled through human mechanization. Then artifice takes over and the scene is duly reset. With motorized precision, the models slide back to their starting positions. This is perhaps the strangest and most heart-wrenching part of the program, and it is this industrious backsliding, complete with the creaking wheels of machinery concealed beneath the fur, that reminds me indelibly of your music.

RECEPTION

The words of the station master moved us deeply, stirring up long dormant emotions of humility and shame. Stealing away to our favorite haunts, we revisited the highs and lows of his implied critique. At times he seemed like a gregarious father figure, eager to take us under his wing by confessing the sordid details of his formative years. At other times he gave way to sheer meanspiritedness, scalding our tender hides with his blistering pronouncements. A week passed as we tried to discern his true feelings toward us and uncover the hidden meaning of his message. Though his words were largely unflattering, we found ourselves smiling inwardly, secretly rejoicing at having our creations listened to and considered.

Holding onto this last vestige of hope, we set about composing an agreeable reply to his e-mail. How could we express our feelings without offending him? How could we ever match his largesse? With trepidation, we eked out a first attempt:

> Forgive this clumsy reply, for all our expressions are inadequate in the face of your extraordinary communiqué. Truly we are unworthy of your mentorship, undeserving of your edification and counsel. Yet here we sit hunched over our keyboard, stringing together mere words of admiration, as we consider the hapless beginnings that marked your

We broke off abruptly, appalled by our obsequious opening. Discarding the draft and starting anew, we tried for a more personal approach:

> After reading your message, we were rendered speechless, overcome by a flood of thoughts and unable to go about our daily tasks. It's only after a week that we can begin to formulate a response, in an effort to bridge the underlying distance between us.

> Will you permit a confession? Two, maybe three weeks ago, we spotted you waiting in line at the drugstore, a jug of burgundy and some ballpoint pens in your shopping basket. You were wearing a sweatshirt and baggy jeans and your guard was down, as if you were in a place where you wouldn't be recognized or judged and could just be yourself. We watched you discreetly from the magazine racks, mesmerized by our unexpected sighting. Your movements were natural and unrehearsed and there was a general air of openness and vulnerability about you; the slope of your shoulders suggested tiredness or an acquaintance with defeat. Already, we had embraced you as our guide. But in that moment, we began to see you as a person. And now after your epic note, we feel sympathy and comprehension. We understand why your gaze was cast downward, why you gripped the handles of your basket with such residual longing.

> Suddenly you looked up, alerted by some invisible sign, some mysterious change in the atmosphere that you couldn't see or identify. Then the moment passed and your face relaxed again. Could you sense our presence, the intoxication of your fans behind the velvet rope? Day after day, we've felt the force of your influence, the intensity of your persona over the radio waves. Tell us, have you sensed us on the other end, listening back?

We wrote the letter in one headlong rush of passion and reread it with tender feeling. But in the end we were embarrassed by its romantic overtones and decided not to send it. Opening a new window, we typed a few hurried lines and shut our eyes tight before hitting the send button:

Dear Sir,

Thank you for considering our work. We appreciate the depth of your response and hope to win your esteem in the future. :-)

Best regards,
The Ambient Parkers

The next few nights were spent in sleepless anxiety, as we tossed and turned with regret over our hasty message. Did we dare hope for an ongoing correspondence with the station master? Had we committed a fatal error with our vapid emoticon? Cursing the smiley face and other hieroglyphics of modern-day communication, we vowed to redeem ourselves in the eyes of our formidable mentor. Like newly enrolled students, we dedicated ourselves over the next twelve weeks to the station master and his life lessons.

Days passed without further word from the station master but we felt little discouragement, so absorbed were we by our new activities. We checked out stacks of opera CDs from the public library, thumbing through the lengthy librettos, singing along to the arias with our reedy voices and faulty Italian. In the history section, we stumbled upon the salacious, tell-all memoir of a promiscuous soprano and her long-suffering manservant. Reciting passages of smut and intrigue late into the night, we schooled ourselves in their romantic crises and existential disappointments. In the morning, with our backpacks full of books and audio recordings, we journeyed to the refuge of individual armchairs, reliving the station master's global travels and tracking his path toward an uncertain enlightenment.

Our coursework tested our commitment and rewarded us with the knowledge that we had, if nothing else, employed the public library's resources with success. Armed with the vague sense of having attained an honorary degree, we set off in search of postgraduate work. The sounds of barking in a neighboring suite gave us an idea. We cleared out our spare room, visited the local animal shelter, and adopted a puppy and middle-aged dog, both with engaging temperaments. Their spirited yips and yelps distracted us from our habitual melancholia. Soon we felt an affectionate joy in their games, a feeling of vicarious achievement in the well-chewed sticks and moist tennis balls retrieved with happy abandon. As we tended to their needs with routine acts of devotion, our lives acquired grace and meaning.

Turning once again to our recordings, we began rearranging old cuts and constructing new ones to fill in the gaps of what was becoming our first concept album. With an eye to early retirement, our eldest member declared himself our manager and threw himself into the project of jump-starting our stalled career. Sporting a new tie and blazer, he was the picture of verve and determination. Within the month, he established contact with a number of rising stars and pivotal players in the greater music world. One evening at the head of the dinner table, he forked up the last of his kale and set down his napkin solemnly. Utilizing a toothpick to prolong the moment of suspense, he announced that we had signed with a local record label with a reputation for championing indie acts and sharpening the outermost edge of the mainstream.

While our manager met with studio reps to renegotiate our contract on better terms, we loitered by the vending machines, browsing the arrays of sodas and salty snacks. Strident voices leaked out through the glass walls of the conference room, where he could be seen rolling his eyes and pounding the table in bouts of bravado. After two hours of passionate speechifying and deal busting, he finally emerged flushed and triumphant. He led us out of the building, reached into his inner coat pocket, and whisked out a handwritten check for a fifty-percent advance.

With our coffers replenished, we could no longer cite financial insolvency as the sole roadblock to completing our album. Under the guidance of our manager, we abandoned our lazy habits and kept to a rigorous schedule of sound assembly and rework. Fixing a red pencil behind his ear in the manner of an accountant, he directed and intimidated us, propelling us along a trajectory of visible progress. When we lost steam, he was right there by our sides, inspiring us with the latest pop-psych mumbo jumbo and key passages from Baudelaire's expositions on Poe.

Transformed into cogs of mass production, we bore down on our task and turned out two hundred and fifty-three minutes of driving ambient noise, which we cut down to seventy-five minutes over several weeks of intense studio sessions. The cover art was spare, consisting of a blurred crimson shadow overlaid with our album title in somber black type. In place of liner notes, we inserted Polaroids of the sites where our recordings had originated. Listeners who picked up our disc would be struck first by the images of depopulated postindustrial zones and then by the collection of songs that would narrate a strange, glacial procession through these damaged dream zones—a haunting soundtrack to a postmortem of the natural world.

Our album was released in the spring to the deafening silence of the public. Urged on by our manager, we held anemic signings at record stores and granted interviews to lackluster radio personalities, who kept fidgeting in their seats and mispronouncing the titles of our songs. Bearing the cross of those who serve up reality over euphemistic fabrication, we braced ourselves for the onset of poverty that would surely follow our disappointing sales. Our one consolation was the darkness that descended upon our suite each night, relieving us from the sight of our manager combing the want ads and calling our attention to openings for local waitstaff. In our despair, we considered giving up music altogether, disbanding, and going our separate ways.

Then something shifted in the world of culture and fashion, and the pendulum of popular opinion began to swing in our favor. Crowds squeezed into our postlaunch parties, prompting our engagements to be moved to ever larger and higher-profile venues. People of all stripes approached us to confess that they at first had hated our record with a passion, but now could not stop playing it. The senior music critic of a well-known glossy magazine penned a feature on us, describing our album as "a mask torn from the face of the machine, a spotlight on the global spectacle of greed and waste, a total sonic assault on transnational capital and bourgeois liberal humanism." Even the station master came around eventually, adding our lesser-known songs to his playlist and conceding on-air that we had made "a minor, not entirely insignificant contribution" to the musical tradition.

Bowled over by the attention, we embarked on a campaign of shameless self-promotion, making media appearances and scoring gigs throughout the region. Dispensing with the banalities of food and sleep, we operated solely on caffeine and the exhilaration of our high. Our private selves were subsumed into the kaleidoscope of our public image, and our public image turned round and round like a new constellation in the star-studded skies. At our manager's prodding, we took our show on the road, loading our equipment into a used Volkswagen bus newly converted to run on biodiesel. Parked outside the entrance of our suite, he tapped its horn twice and opened its rusty side doors with the enthusiasm of a showman. We jostled for seating amidst an overstock of barrels smelling faintly of fried food, our stomachs set into motion.

Our itinerary unfolded before us like a wobbly pen stroke passing through major cities and mid-size towns from coast to coast. The wonders of our nation never ceased to present themselves, as our boxy vehicle puttered along barren multilane highways, strip malls doubling as rest stops, and Main Streets lined with chain stores. In the spirit of group solidarity, we stopped at an art supply store and festooned the outside of our bus with environmental murals, along with opinionated bumper stickers spun from construction paper and tape. Like a circus barker, our manager shouted through a megaphone, announcing our arrival to the locals with tantalizing catchphrases. At loosely arranged times, we parked in abandoned lots and gave unofficial concerts, gathering new fans, curiosity seekers, and police patrols wherever we went.

In a move against boredom, we devised a repertoire of performative shticks to beguile our audiences and keep our concerts interesting. For one show, we hired good-looking actors to carry out our parts while we remained sequestered backstage in sweats, strumming and programming the actual soundtrack. We repeated this stunt the next night, but with the actors dressed like fashion plates, brandishing cell phones and high-pitched keyless remotes in a landscape of strewn hubcaps and fast-food waste. On other occasions, we threw caution to the wind and appeared incognito, using sheets and tie-down rope to portray dashing villains from "I, Claudius." Our toga-party image contrasted sharply with the vibrato of our high-tech tunes, prompting some in the audience to scratch their heads and search for connections between the costumery of one late empire and the musical flights of another.

In between shows, we slung on our day bags and explored the local attractions, noting the subtle differences in window displays between corporate franchises. On our free days, we drove our bus along winding offbeat paths, stopping at diners for greasy-spoon meal deals and trading posts for handicrafts and kitschy knickknacks. Steering our bus alongside designated outlook points, we cut the motor and opened the barn door to reveal the majestic expanse of mountains and canyons that lay just behind us. We leaned back against the cases and crates of our cargo to enjoy the scenery, sipping water from reusable bottles and snacking on peanuts, the shells collecting at our feet.

Fields of poppies called out to us, and there was scarcely a swimming hole or forbidden reservoir that did not see our naked glistening forms, as we stripped down to the buff for an impulsive skinny-dip or waddle in the cool, clean water. Happy in our recreation, deaf to the catcalls and dog whistles of passing motorists, we sunbathed au naturel on the rocks, our faces turned up to the bright blue sky, our toes wagging in the manner of innocents traveling abroad in our own unspoiled heartland.

The wilderness awed us with its ceaseless variety and dramatic changes in scale. Moved to dust off our tripod, we trained our camera lens on panoramic vistas and pincushion beds of wildflowers. Once the photography bug bit us, other bucolic hobbies soon followed. Birdwatching, outdoor watercolor painting, and amateur gemology occupied us in turn. Like Atkinson and Nabokov, we took up lepidopterology but only as observers, following the paths of rare butterflies over verdant meadows and wildwood brambles.

These idyllic pursuits soothed our spirits, transporting us back to an era of simpler pleasures and slower tempos: before the microchip, before the combustion engine, before the electrical wire with its transmissions of charge and overload. We wound down like tired machines, sounding off before idling. A lazy drawl crept into our speech as we read nature guides and chewed on leaves of grass. At twilight, we pitched tents by the side of the road, cooking over a campfire as the night came alive with a chorus of crickets and frogs. After supper, we lay under the stars and dreamt of returning to our primeval origins: from hand to paw, paw to flipper, flipper to plankton, plankton to sedimentary slush—to the explosive beginnings of the earth and its first blazing sunrise.

Sadly, our halcyon summer days were destined to end. As we left the two-lane highway, we crested a mountaintop overlooking a burgeoning valley laid waste to house modern man and his upright developments. Skylines and billboards hastened our return to the fold. We became nervous and tense again, our senses assailed by the never-ending flux of traffic and people. Back at the studio Monday afternoon, we attended an all-hands meeting where our manager reviewed our goals and handed out a calendar of new media engagements. Stepping out to meet our professional obligations, we squared our shoulders and fixed our gaze straight ahead, trading moon glow for slick city lights, lo-fi dreams for studio hustle.

To reconnect with our public, we became virtual shut-ins. Unwashed in rumpled pajamas, we lowered the blinds and stationed ourselves at the desk, where our thoughts intermingled with the flickering computer screen and whining fax machine. As we made our way through a bag of stale jujubes, we checked e-mail for the first time since returning from our trip, balking at the alert indicating one thousand-plus new messages. Working steadily over the next week, we tackled our inbox and took it down to just five messages: a reminder for an upcoming dental cleaning and the rest pure unadulterated fan mail. Ignoring modern communication trends, we replied to each fan with thought, feeling, and other personal touches.

As the month passed with dwindling public appearances, we loafed on the couch or slipped outside to a folding chair for a nap, while our manager grew sulky and irascible. A herald of our uncertain financial future, he took to pacing the halls of our suite with dramatically turned-out pockets. At an impromptu meeting, he urged us to strike while the iron was hot, pressing us to become a household name, a brand the listening public could flaunt like the one-hundred-dollar logo on an article of yuppie sportswear. To emphasize his point, he held up one of his smelly running shoes, an unsightly wad of gum stuck to its tread. Motioning us to the office with clenched teeth, he offered us seats around the desk, powered on the computer, and firmly shut the door.

Downloading and transmitting data at go-go rates, we hurled ourselves into the matterless space of the Internet, gravitating ever closer to the heart of the buzz. On popular social networking sites, we created elaborate profiles of our band rife with half-truths and made glamorous with digital snapshots of ourselves on the road. We friended influential journalists with our honed wit and watched our follower count surge with our on-line celebrity clashes. Our daily tweets and shout-outs resulted in constant attention, a fomenting mix of adulation and loathing. As the culmination to this tour de force, we took up an on-line residency in a utopian artists' collective cosponsored by anarchists, intellectuals, and the French—a green tome embossed with a raised fist welcoming visitors to its home page.

When a prominent blogger posted a glowing review of our album amounting to a benediction, we found ourselves catapulted to new echelons of celebrity. We became the next It band, the artists of the moment, the people to see and be seen with. Offers came pouring in by the droves. New fans started up tribute sites and zines in our name, while old fans folded their publications in disgust, convinced that we had lost our integrity and sold out to the Man. Social cliques that had once seemed impossibly out of our league now opened their doors to us, inviting us to exclusive parties and subsidizing our appearances with bags of merchandise from event sponsors.*

Keeping up with the local glitterati, we abandoned our suite and moved into a spacious loft near the waterfront. In addition to unprecedented fame, we experienced a dramatic rise in our sex appeal. Spurred on by winks and nudges from our manager, we learned to reap the benefits of guaranteed allure and carefree seduction. Working the scene at after-show gatherings, we flirted shamelessly and went home with our best-looking admirers. Our utopian residency was curtailed, our energies channeled into a string of midafternoon hookups and weekend dalliances. On our free nights, we lounged in the VIP booths of smoky underground bars, toying and romping with the vixens and studs of landed bohemia.

Our young-and-hot period lasted exactly seven weeks, five days, and fourteen hours. During this phase, we flopped on recliner mattresses and vibrator beds, running up outlandish hotel bills and shedding extra pounds from the recreational exercise. We

---

* Soon after, an invitation packet to a rock-'n'-roll winter wonderland arrived in our mailbox with pictures of last year's singers and musicians tripped out in gold chains and rings, fur-lined parkas and boots displaying a morbid oneness with coyotes, foxes, raccoons, rabbits, and other beleaguered wildlife. In the photos, names and logos of event sponsors appeared prominently on buildings, walls, kegs, and glassware. Meanwhile, celebrities hugged corporate reps and held up their latest tech-gadget must-haves with million-dollar smiles before the kneeling paparazzi. To preserve our dignity, we shredded the fulsome packet and others like it before our manager caught wind of them.

experimented with alternative looks, picking out the mood of the moment from our newly expanded wardrobe, from designer sport coats and ripped jeans, to nerd glasses and buttoned-up shirts, to skintight tops and microminis. Steamy assignations became commonplace and orgies flared up as quickly as tempers on a hot summer's day. We flew into reckless pleasure zones, riding high in the sky with money in our pockets and a gleam in our eye, until gravity kicked in and yanked us down to the mundane. As our fair-weather lovers parachuted to safety, we plummeted to the earth like misguided pilots, awakening to the rude reality of our lumpy physiques and premature decrepitude.

Although our loss of appeal came as something of a letdown, we seized the opportunity to catch up on our beauty sleep while our manager redefined our goals. Donning a smoking jacket, he now spent the evenings gazing out at the bay, sipping a glass of port, and writing in a journal. One night he led us up to the roof, passed around a few bottles of cheap champagne, and raised his hand in silence. His hair blowing wildly in the wind, he flipped through his diary to dog-eared pages and cited passages that foretold of our future: a series of ambitious side projects that we would launch using our album's success as a springboard.

Over the next three months, we DJ-ed several opening-night parties at an up-and-coming art gallery in gentrified downtown; founded a music festival centered around ambient noise and collage; launched a record label for bands discovered through our festival; put up the seed money for a scholarship to be awarded annually to music students demonstrating exceptional talent in the field of ambient composition; published articles in major newspapers hinting at the emergence of a broad cultural movement now forming in our name; and posted an on-line manifesto heralding Ambient Parking as the antidote to all that was stale and lifeless in experimental music, as well as the basis for deep structural change in the areas of transportation, resource management, education, and the ethics of daily life.

We attracted much attention with our upstart polemics. Seasoned critics pooh-poohed our claims, while other bands accused us of grandstanding and cultural profiteering. Our fans were divided in their opinions. Some celebrated our call to action, organizing affinity groups and flash mobs to carry out the proposals set forth in our manifesto. Others expressed their disapproval by boycotting our shows and chastising us for publicity-seeking pseudointellectualism. With calculated poise, we held ourselves aloof from both camps, forging through our performances without comment and allowing our silent mystique to ripen and grow.

One day as we played to a mixed crowd at a neighborhood street fair, we were interrupted by the noisy rattling of a chain-link fence. A gang of young toughs from the university jumped over at once and challenged us to defend our manifesto. When we tried to ignore them, they grew rowdy and aggressive, shouting aphorisms by well-known theorists until we were forced to lower our instruments and rebut them on the spot. After fifteen minutes of heated insults and throw-downs, we exchanged solemn handshakes and agreed to settle our differences through a civilized debate in the graduate studies hall.

Over the next week and a half, we crammed incessantly for the academic showdown, absorbing Cliff's Notes on critical theory and combing through select papers. With nervously churning stomachs, we copied out flash cards of key terms and concepts, quizzing one another intensely under conditions of mock interrogation. To camouflage our ignorance, we cultivated agile speech patterns and compiled an arsenal of quick-witted comebacks. We studied video footage of the great Oxford debates, taking note of the clever ploys and rhetorical sleights of hand that could be used to impress and intimidate. When the fateful day arrived, we strode into the hall ten minutes early, armed with crisp cheat sheets and dressed to the nines.

The auditorium was packed with an assembly of our supporters and detractors. At the back of the room were the undergraduates, all of them young and green, a few wearing concert T-shirts from our tour, who clapped and cheered when we entered. The middle rows were filled with a loose conglomerate of stone-faced doctoral candidates and their hipster counterparts, while the gentle men and women of the press occupied the ringside seats with notepads in hand, ready to memorialize every pea-brained remark and scandalous slip of the tongue. Looming in the wings were scads of curiosity seekers and at least one Nobel laureate. Our student challengers were already onstage, sitting behind an oblong table equipped with detachable mikes, scowling and spoiling for a fight. Sauntering up the aisle, we took our seats behind the adjacent table and whisked off our dark glasses.

The rules of engagement were simple: five open-ended questions posed to each team in turn by the moderator, with time allotted for rebuttals and a free sally of retorts. The winner would be determined by the audience through popular vote. In addition to notepads, pens, and half-pints of water, each team was supplied with a faculty advisor—a tenured professor with a keen interest in the issues at stake—who would offer guidance and intervene if matters got out of hand.

The sponsor for the opposing team was a living academic legend, a cheerful, strapping fellow in horn-rims who had emerged in the late 1980s as something of a teenage prodigy and penned the first draft of his dissertation in just twenty-five days. Since then, he had published numerous influential screeds on mass media and popular culture, along with a series of pocket-sized pamphlets that disseminated his theories to professionals and laymen alike. He divided his time between Los Angeles, New York, and Tel Aviv, where he assumed a variety of guest teaching positions and had, it was said, a satisfied lover in every port.

By comparison, we balked when presented with our own advisor, a severe, beaky-nosed individual who was all tics and twitches, dressed in an ill-fitted tweed suit that left his gangly wrists exposed. The gawkiness of his demeanor, however, belied his shrewd mental powers. We were pleasantly surprised by the breadth and relevance of his credentials: he had authored a well-respected monograph on "Information Architecture and the Cultural Capital of Attention"; he had received a Pew grant as well as a MacArthur fellowship for his enlarged photographs of shoppers strolling the aisles of American supermarkets; and one of his poetic shopping lists had been nominated for a Pushcart prize. When he spoke, his awkward features coalesced into an appealing whole and his ideas flowed forth with astonishing eloquence.

With the rapping of a gavel, the debate began. We fielded the first question deftly, thwarting our opponents' attack with solid arguments and spirited rhetoric. The mixed response—some heckling and some applause—signaled to us that the skirmish had resulted in a draw. In response to the second question, we picked up our instruments and played a downtempo acoustic version of "Ambient Parking #25." The entire assembly fell silent and looked on raptly. Our loyal contingent swayed in time to the languid beat, and when we lifted our heads at the end of the performance, we saw a soft cloud of dreamy smiles materialize in the audience, obscuring the frowns of our detractors.

After a moment's delay, our challengers sprang back to life, flinging down their pens and accusing us of "drugging the masses with sound-derived opiates." They lambasted our technique and denounced our aesthetic. Finally, they leapt to the front of the stage and unfurled a gigantic swath of white butcher paper. The scroll was entitled the "Arc of Cultural Production" and presented a timeline of cultural milestones in black with a thick stroke of red ink above it. This heroic bloodline soared through the centuries, periodically dipping and then surging up again during the Crusades, the Renaissance, and Romanticism. It peaked around Modernism, which also marked the first of many schisms. After this, the red line fared poorly, fragmenting through Postmodernism and the Death of the Subject until it smashed head-on with Identity Politics and Revisionist Critique. Here the graph broke off abruptly and the carnage resulting from this late cultural collision was pushed discreetly out of sight, somewhere past the boundaries of the scroll.

At the far end of the graph near one of its steepest ravines, the student dogmatists now drew an offshoot line, around which they sketched a cluster of contemporary movements, enclosed in misshapen bubbles reminiscent of tumorous growths. With surgical precision, they located and identified the Transparently Self-Serving, Delusionary Radical, Unforgivably Inane, and Prematurely Triumphalist. At the center of this diseased area, they placed a sickly green dot. This speck, they claimed, represented the full range of influence that we could realistically hope to exert on the greater culture with our music.

A general uproar ensued, the entire hall clamoring to speak up at once. Unnerved by our opponents' low blows but refusing to be harassed by their Venn diagram, we added our voices to the mix, shouting and retorting at top volume until the moderator pounded the gavel and called the room to order. A brief intermission was announced, and we followed the streaming crowd to a well-stocked refreshment table.

After calming our nerves with plastic tumblers of merlot, we parked ourselves near the cheese platter to observe the intelligentsia at work. A few were engaged in lively discourse, no doubt provoked by the onstage controversy. But most simply milled about with crumpled napkins in hand, looking lost and disoriented. Budding scholars approached peers with their pet theories, only to be put off by blank looks and barely suppressed yawns.

An impromptu gathering of students had formed around the two faculty luminaries, who appeared to be expounding upon a matter of great import. The acolytes hung on their every word and alteration in facial expression, nodding reverently and smiling at key moments. Longing to be privy to this momentous dialogue, we moved within earshot, only to discover that the professors were merely trading notes on their favorite five-star restaurants. Their conversation touched upon various gastronomic delights, with a pronounced difference of opinion on fusion appetizers and nouveau cuisine.

With quietly gurgling stomachs, we reassembled for round two of the debate. Although we had steeled ourselves for fierce intellectual combat, our preparations proved unnecessary. Our team advisor seized the microphone and began expertly debunking the other side's claims on our behalf. Grinning arrogantly, his rival promptly took up the challenge.

For several minutes, the professors cautiously circled each other in speech, sending out verbal feelers to size each other up. Occasionally, one would thrust a sharp point or idea into the air, the other would follow suit, and the two points would come into contact. A series of quick parries would ensue, as the scholars deflected each other's attacks with witty ripostes and clever quips. With the audience captivated by the duel, we settled back in our chairs, relieved that our cause was finally being championed by a seasoned advocate.

The games were a pleasure to watch, as invigorating as a day by the seaside. Like an inflatable beach ball, the subject of our music was bounced back and forth by the professors, from one side of the argument to the other. Our sponsor touted us as antinomian products of a post-Fordist society, while his colleague derided us as poster children for the status quo. After several such exchanges, they tossed us aside and moved on to larger concerns, while the idea of Ambient Parking rolled away like a forgotten toy.

With this crucial shift in terms, the debate turned tense and serious. In tandem with the audience, we leaned forward on the edges of our seats, bracing ourselves for an ideological brawl. As a palpable pressure filled the hall, whopping ideas came raining down and the storm commenced. The academic titans clashed onstage with deafening blows, grappling on the craggy shore of criticism that marked the university's outer limits. Like a discarded argument, we bobbed helplessly in the sea of undiscovered knowledge, waves surging and crashing all around us.

By the grace of Providence, we were scooped up by an invisible hand and tossed to the safety of the beach, where we awaited the outcome of the showdown amidst a crowd of spectators. From this new vantage point, our insignificance in the academic world became clear to us. Our music had been a mere ploy for setting the real debate into motion, a piece of cultural evidence that could be used to prop up one critic's theory or the other's. As artists, we were superfluous to the discourse. Even the tough-talking students who had challenged us initially were shown to be voluntary pawns of the system, junior grunts following strategic loyalties and affiliations of power, all with the aim of hustling up the hierarchy of command and seizing the helm of scholarship one day for themselves.

The final verdict was inconclusive. Half the audience voted for us, while the other half favored our opponents. When the moderator pronounced the contest a draw, the room erupted in light applause amid a chorus of boos and hisses. Our sponsor reached across the table and pumped our arms up and down, vowing to celebrate our triumph in one of his forthcoming essays. Confounded by his victorious attitude, we grew even more puzzled when his rival strode over to slap us on the back and thank us for handing him an easy win. Only the student challengers failed to disguise their displeasure, their downcast faces conceding defeat.

Soon after, an academic journal wrapped in a brown envelope arrived in our mailbox, containing the promised mention from our sponsor. Within weeks, we were inducted into the canon of the moment. Our recordings were invoked at symposiums and conferences, our manifesto anthologized in class readers for courses in music appreciation and environmental aesthetics. Trendsetting intellectuals competed to name-drop our album in their latest articles, while spirited discussions of our discography could be heard in the coffeehouses bordering ivy-trimmed campuses. On occasion we would disguise ourselves as café busybodies, jumping into these conversations to correct minor points or offer a guiding hand.

Our scaling of the ivory tower was accompanied by a precipitous decline in our street cred. A-list clubs dropped us from their calendars, influential rock journalists neglected to return our calls, and even the electronic music nerds shook us off at parties. Faux college diplomas, rolled up and ribboned to conceal words of hate, began arriving at our doorstep. To make matters worse, hefty books had lately been aimed at the stage during our performances, from the *Riverside Chaucer* to *Nigella Bites*. Sitting in the kitchen with ice packs pressed to bruised shins, we felt momentarily cheered when one of our hits came streaming out from the radio, only to hear the announcer disparaging the song as "elitist driving music."

Dazed and demoralized, we holed up in our loft and shut our ears against the hostile noise. We filled our time with layperson's yoga, watching our dogs closely and emulating their positions throughout the loft. We pulled out our stash of letters from the scholars who wished to conduct research on us, vacillating for several days before agreeing to their demands. We unearthed photos and souvenirs from our glory days, revisiting fond memories of the street-corner gigs and amphitheater shows where our songs had once been embraced by the minor masses.

Despite our best efforts, a postpartum depression wormed into our being. We grew listless and uninspired, incapable of playing our instruments or holding our recording mike with any trace of enthusiasm. Tears welled up in our eyes seemingly without rhyme or reason, spilling out when we went about our daily tasks. When our own record label threatened to oust us from its board of directors for "causing an academic brouhaha" and "alienating the man on the street," we stepped down preemptively and resigned from our other side projects.

Desperate for us to make a fresh start, our manager flipped through his Rolodex and combed the local phone book, searching for a miracle worker to cure our malaise. After an extended conversation with the director of a local sanitarium, he was referred to a team of motivational coaches specializing in whole-person makeovers for has-been celebrities. Before long, the professionals installed themselves comfortably in our quarters, where they subjected us to their ministrations for a steep hourly fee.

A daily agenda was soon established. We were roused each morning at dawn by our fitness coach, who whistle-hounded us around a nearby track on sprints and conditioning runs. Following a barrage of sit-ups and push-ups, we sat down for a sensible breakfast of yogurt and fruit, watching attentively as the nutritionist preweighed our noontime portions on a small platform scale. Our wardrobe consultant assembled smart-looking outfits from the offerings in our closet, while a senior aesthetician tutored us in the finer points of hair and skin care. Neatly coiffed and dressed, we convened in the common room for the first of the day's group therapy sessions.

Prodded by our therapist, we struggled to individuate, to venture out from the protective shelter of "we" and stand unassisted in the light. Most of us failed the test, buckling at the knees and crawling back to the safety of the fold. A few members, however, managed to voice their true feelings and wrench free of the codependent mass. Self-help and daily meditation books collected on their bedside tables. Later during candid interviews with the house videographer, they shared their secret fears and breakthroughs, as the rest of us closed ranks reflexively and looked on with deep-seated resentment.

Like caterpillars we wriggled in our skins, awaiting our transformation. After twelve weeks of intensive beautification and moderate self-recovery, we emerged from our cocoons and stretched our wings with delight. Outside, the world looked bright and full of promise, the faces of people warm and accepting. We entered a public park with our dogs in the lead, smiling at passersby. Following a paved footpath, we found ourselves overlooking a grassy incline dotted with park-goers on blankets, some fast asleep, some staring thoughtfully into the distance.

And now in the anonymous babble of the park, we thought we could hear a voice speaking to us—a voice from the past, remote yet familiar, reaching out from afar, resounding through the crowds and avenues to find us, its volume muted and identity unknown. We could almost recognize its singular hesitations, its impetuous stops and starts, its way of beginning answers with questions, along with its questioning mood in general. As the seconds ticked by, the reception improved.

Resting beside one of the blankets was a black box, a portable stereo with an extended antenna. Shaded by a small striped umbrella, someone was listening to the radio broadcast of an interview with the voice, which we now recognized as that of our collaborator from long ago, the dancer whom we had directed by slow degrees to die in a wrecked automobile. Since that fateful night her career had blossomed and matured, and she had given many other extreme performances: solo gymnastics on the girders of a windy telecommunications tower (Chicago), a three-part balancing act on the rim of a wooden tub in a women's bathhouse (Osaka), and depictions of affliction on the loading deck of an aerial parking structure (Kuala Lumpur), to name but a few. In the interview, she was soft-spoken yet assured, just as we remembered her. And it took only a few moments of listening for us to realize that she remembered us too.

DEATH OF AN AUTOMOTIVE DANCER

Radio host: How did you meet the Ambient Parkers?

Dancer: [*Clears her throat*] It's hard to say exactly. I'd been dragged to a couple of their shows by a friend of mine, a budding art collector with lots of free time on his hands and an eye for the down-and-out. On other occasions, I'd watched them from a distance at the after-parties connected with the performance scene that was happening at the time. The band had become recognizable to me by then, although their features could be described as quite ordinary. As individuals, they could have gone unnoticed in a room full of quirky, vivacious people chatting, gossiping, flirting, and networking at top speed—all the artsy go-getters with a million projects to finish, a million people to see. By contrast, each member of the Ambient Parkers looked more like a sulky wallflower, crossing the floor alone to the bar or waiting silently in the restroom line. But standing next to one another, they somehow came together as a group, amassing an identity that you couldn't ignore or deny. I'm not saying that they looked particularly united in purpose—no, quite the opposite. What they shared most was an air of distraction, a sense of foreboding that came through in their restless shifting and quiet shuffling, which contrasted sharply with the frenetic energy around them.

RH: How did you come to be at these parties?

D: Oh, I was a competent player on the scene, more or less. I performed my part well, one that might be summarized as: girl from the rural Northwest moves to the big city to study comparative literature; drops out after five semesters due to lack of discipline and funds; tries her hand at various jobs like house painting, waiting tables, and palm reading; has a few boyfriends along the way, none very serious or good-looking, but all the decent sort; stumbles upon a group of dancers with an interest in hybrid performance; obsessively attends every show seen advertised or heard about by word of mouth; makes new friends; gets evicted from her teacup studio apartment via the Ellis Act; moves into a ramshackle, multilevel Victorian with a cooperative of self-identified artists; discovers that her compact build and early gymnastics training enables her to execute maneuvers that would be physically impossible for the average person; and gradually makes a name for herself as a dancer with an inclination toward the minimalist and conceptual.

RH: Would you say that you, unlike the Ambient Parkers, fit in at these parties then?

D: Actually, I'd grown somewhat dissatisfied with my role in that community and the sight of this band of misfits always gave me a burst of hope. I was beginning to feel confined by the part I'd created for myself, the part I'd practiced and perfected and was now expected to perform—day or night, rain or shine—not for my own sake but for everyone else's. In order to survive, the scene depended on the maintaining of a delicate equilibrium between its participants—a careful balancing act between all kinds of characters and personalities, loyalties and enmities, friends and lovers, scandals and breakups. In this sense, it was no different from any other closed social system. It was a society of mutual patronage, governed by courtly rules and favors. At the height of my participation, I likened it to the belle monde circles that I'd read about in the pages of Tolstoy and Proust, a twenty-four-hour salon party hosted in living rooms and venues scattered across the city.

Just like in those worlds, the people in my circle could be petty and cruel, caught up in their small jealousies and grudges. It was like high school all over again, high school for adults. Work did come into play, but more as an afterthought; it was one part productivity, three parts career climbing. But in momentary flashes these people could also be grand, capable of rich feelings and expression. They could make amazing things happen because they loved art and believed it had the power to supply what was sorely missing in the world. They believed the ills of life could be improved through creativity, and I believe they were right. I wanted to be a member of that golden club. I wanted to be Pierre, Prince Andrei, or Natasha, holding onto my integrity no matter what, refusing to be drowned in the seas of hypocrisy. But in reality, I was at risk of becoming the Duchess de Guermantes, that society woman who showed more concern over a pair of fashionable shoes than the welfare of her sick and dying friend. I played my part well enough. I met and talked to all the right people, accepted all the right invitations. But at the same time, I sensed something misdirected and empty about my actions, as if by working the scene so shamelessly—schmoozing ad nauseam, drumming up audiences for my shows, chasing after the commissions that would keep me in good professional standing—I was also robbing my art of the one true thing that nourished and sustained it. That's honestly how I felt. I was wracked with guilt practically every day.

RH: You mentioned that seeing the Ambient Parkers gave you hope?

D: [*Laughs*] This is going to sound crazy, but I found myself looking to the Ambient Parkers for reassurance and support. At first I'd catch a glimpse of them by accident, as I peered past my plastic wine glass and over the shoulder of my conversation partner. The band would be milling in the background and I would feel an immediate sense of relief. Later, I would scan the crowd for their faces—those expressionless, pavement faces—and feel disappointed when I failed to locate them. Then the configuration of the room would shift, some people would move off toward the bar and others would arrive to take their place, and they would miraculously appear before me, clumped together with their fists closed tightly around photocopied program notes or zines. I'd watch them make their way to the stairwell leading up to the roof, where the most mental types liked to congregate and converse, hypothesizing about anything and everything under the sun, lingering by a low cement wall overlooking a fatal drop to the heart of the city, hanging on by loose threads of talk and perpetually half-finished drinks till the wee hours of morning. As the band swept past me, grazing my shoulder in their drab overcoats, I would be struck with feelings of affinity and homeyness. I would stand a little taller and feel a little brighter, convinced that I was no longer alone in the world.

RH: What did you see in them?

D: I had a feeling you'd ask me that. Would it surprise you if I said it was their identification with their source? They had the silliest premise to begin with, as you know. Parking lots, multilevel garages, cars pulling in and out. Some vague thesis about the environment, overpopulation, and greed. To be honest, I didn't follow these aspects very closely, because I was never that thrilled by their music as *music*, if you know what I mean. Whenever I listened to it, I was unable to distinguish it from the background sounds I heard everyday. [*Shifts in her chair*] It was their relation to their work that moved me, not just their overall stance but the level of intimacy they maintained with their source materials. At the time, there were all kinds of crazy stories circulating about them. They had made themselves homeless for their art, living for four months out of a borrowed station wagon which they parked in a corporate garage, bribing the parking attendants to leave them in peace as they moved the car over to the next marked stall every night, until they had systematically occupied every single space in the garage—a total of one hundred sixteen spaces, including the disabled spaces and stalls reserved for motorcycles and mopeds. Apparently, they had created nightly recordings for every space, but refused to release the tracks to the public or reproduce them instrumentally during shows because, in their own alleged words, "these recordings were meant to be made, not heard." What can you say in the face of such claims? I don't know if any of this was true, but it certainly contributed to the air of mystique that enveloped them.

Do you see what I mean? I was moved because they refused to be moved by prevailing cultural currents and social pressures. They didn't budge and they rarely compromised. They identified so closely with their source that they were totally willing to disappear into it, to become as pavement-faced as their materials, to relinquish their authorship to the asphalt. Naturally, this impressed me because of my own overdependence on the scene. I was always following the latest hype or controversy, never putting anything out there that wasn't guaranteed to win the approval of my peers. I knew plenty of people who understood what they wanted— professional success, minor celebrity, a bevy of admirers—and went about making exactly the kind of art that would secure those rewards. But the Ambient Parkers went at it with a totally different approach. They poured all their energies into the art they wanted to make and left it at that; how they came across to others was inconsequential. As you can imagine, this gave them a somewhat aloof, self-absorbed air—not like some of my friends who pouted and swaggered about in a state of indefinite adolescence, but in the manner of medieval anchorites who willfully sequestered themselves in a devotional forest (a devotional forest of parked cars!) in order to hear.

To my mind, the artist they most resembled was Glenn Gould, who famously thought of himself as more a recording artist than a performing artist. I used to listen to Gould's recording of the *Goldberg Variations* regularly, either the youthful, idiosyncratic 1955 version or the later more introverted 1981 version. As I listened, I'd recall Thomas Bernhard's description of Gould in *The Loser* and imagine Gould huddled over the keyboard, tucking into those brilliant chords, humming his ghostly overtones, and withdrawing from the world into his music. In Bernhard's words, he sank into himself and looked "first like an animal, then like a cripple, and finally like the sharp-witted, beautiful man that he was." Seeing the Ambient Parkers loitering in the backdrop of these parties, I would feel strangely connected to them through what I had read of Gould's playing, and I would feel in that moment that we were all blessed and protected from harm. Two words would come to mind: conviction and sanctuary. [*Coughs and takes a drink*]

I'm talking, of course, about the Ambient Parkers in the early part of their career before their big album success, when they were still relatively unknown. They've changed since then, reinvented themselves many times over and slackened many of their original principles.

RH: Before your collaboration with the Ambient Parkers had you ever spoken with them?

D: Just once. I had a conversation with one of the musicians on her own, apart from the rest of the band. It's a funny story, actually.

It happened in the kitchen of a cramped bay-side apartment that had been converted into a performance space for an enormous wandering womb. Various symptoms of hysteria were enacted as the uterine mass moved through rooms representing different regions of the allegorical body of Woman. A climactic act was expected to transpire when it entered the bedchamber and attached to the brain. I didn't stay long enough to witness that harrowing event, but I did experience the unruly organ in the kitchen, or chest cavity, where I stood awestruck with a handful of onlookers as it came sailing toward us like a formidable creature of the sea, all heft and lobe and painted surface.

The sculpture had been filled with helium and required the artists' continuous presence to support it: one at each fallopian tube and a third stationed at the rear to help steer and propel it. As the assemblage drew near the kitchen, it appeared placid and subdued, tricking many of us into lowering our guard. Without warning, the previously well-behaved organ went into some kind of fit, shoving several people, including the one Ambient Parker, into my path. She apologized, and we both laughed in spite of ourselves. We talked for maybe ten minutes and then drifted off in separate directions. And although her features looked familiar to me, I failed to place her as one of the band until I pointed her out weeks later to my art collector friend, who promptly identified her as the regular bass player. Later, when our groups started working together, we acknowledged our prior encounter with confidential smiles, recalling our fleeting moment of intimacy. By that time, I had forgotten her name and she may have forgotten mine, but I'm sure she'd agree that these were just details in the overall scheme of things.

This is all to say that the Ambient Parkers were anything but total strangers when they approached me and asked if I would like to engage in a piece of experimental torture. [*Groans*] Actually, those weren't quite the words they used; they might have said "politicized avant-gardism" or "art with a critical conscience," but you get the idea.

RH: Tell me more about that time, when you first spoke with the Ambient Parkers about your collaboration.

D: The band approached me in the living room of a mutual acquaintance and I must have hesitated before answering, because a look of shyness and self-protection swept over them. "Yes, yes of course, I would love to," I blurted out, surprised they had read my wishes so clearly. Now it was their turn to be surprised. Have you ever been in a deserted parking lot, just looking for a quiet place to sit and mind your own thoughts, watching the sun dip by slow degrees below the horizon, turning orange, then crimson, then violet, when all of a sudden the overhead lights switch on with a great electrifying thump, drenching the place in a white incandescence? Well, it was like that with the band. When they heard me say yes, their grayish faces flushed and lit up, expressing a tender gratitude I never knew they had in them. At first I admit that I was flattered by their vulnerability, but later, lying awake night after night, it frightened me.

It was the beginning of spring after all, about a year and a half after the surprise attacks that would ultimately lead to a full-blown invasion and occupation on the other side of the world. Some of the artists had quit the scene, channeling their energies into political rallies and protests. Others like myself stayed on, holding onto our art with a viselike grip. [*Sighs*] In retrospect, none of us knew what we were taking on. In the greater context of life, we were consummate beginners, just kids really. We had a natural group affinity, a natural feel for the group effort that we needed in order to achieve our goals. And in many ways, this camaraderie enlarged and defined us as artists, but in other ways it held us back, causing us to collapse inwardly and regress emotionally. Many people who were part of the scene held themselves aloof from others and the Ambient Parkers were no different. They invented elaborate distractions to keep themselves busy; they devised painstaking strategies to keep their music spontaneous and unpredictable. In other words, they had fashioned some very effective suits of armor, which insulated and protected them as they went tramping through their parking lots. And like many heavily armored people, they were unusually soft inside, just aching for the chance to reveal this secret part of themselves, the right moment to cast off their defenses and throw themselves open to an experience that they were totally unprepared to handle.

RH: I want to hear more about your collaboration. But before we move on, could you talk a little about your goals at the time as a dancer?

D: Of course. [*Pauses*] For most of my adult life, I had been vaguely aware of something unreal at the core of my persona, a faulty premise teetering on the verge of collapse. It was something like corruption or neglect, or some insidious combination of these two qualities, and I shared it in common with practically everyone I knew. This was the essential material I was working with in my choreographies. And although my greatest aspiration was to someday punch through these qualities and reach their opposites, the most I could do at the time was to go deeper inside the negative material, to amplify it for my audience and draw it out into plain view. If at times my dancing looked torturously slow, if at times I appeared to be at a standstill, it was not for a lack but a surplus of movement. If you watched very closely, you would have seen that I was executing a thousand tiny movements, each one as quick and elusive as a wing beat. And you would have seen how all these tiny movements added up to a single big movement—an invisible leap of faith, as Kierkegaard might have put it.

I lost weight from all the exposure; I became the thinnest dancer imaginable. Given the peculiar nature of my work, it was apparently a struggle just to recognize me. After shows, I'd be approached by people with the most quizzical of expressions on their faces, their eyes blinking rapidly and the corners of their mouths curled up in noncommital half-greetings, which could be tucked away in case I turned out not to be the dancer after all but a mere lookalike. They would tell me that my body seemed to fade with each new set of movements, that I seemed to disappear altogether at times, and that afterward they could barely recall what I looked like, in spite of their very vivid impressions of my choreography. These people would also tell me that whereas their bodies seemed to grow warmer and heavier as the performance progressed, mine seemed to grow colder and lighter, causing some to fear for my health.

RH: Did you ever fear for your health?

D: No. Well, at least not at the time. Although I suppose my collaboration with the Ambient Parkers amounted to a flirtation with death. It was freezing in the cement lot that night, and it took practically everything out of me to sustain the one spark of visceral warmth that I needed to make it through the performance. Perhaps that's all I really wanted, to sustain the temperature of my body, but only *just*.

RH: Earlier, you described your work as "experimental torture." Were the Ambient Parkers aware of what they were asking of you?

D: After I accepted their offer, we discussed some of the broader details of our collaboration and they did make a reference to torture. I immediately latched onto the term because it seemed so crucial to our efforts. "Torture for who?" I ventured. "The audience or ourselves?"

"It all depends on who's in the driver's seat," one of them answered without much thought. The others looked uncomfortable, shifting restlessly. Someone, the keyboardist I think, tried to change the subject, but when he realized that I was waiting for a serious answer, he stopped short.

"It's the nature of my work, you see. I need to know how far we want to take this. Given where we're at right now in history, given the mess our country has gotten itself into, I . . ." I broke off midthought.

"Are you saying you'd like us to sharpen our ideological stance?" someone asked.

"Not exactly," I said, fidgeting with the frayed strands of wool near my feet. By then, we had retreated to a corner of the room and were seated cross-legged on a shabby oriental carpet with a repeating floral pattern, struggling to carry on our conversation as the eternal noises of the party resounded above our heads.

"I guess I'm concerned about falling into the trap of classical drama," I continued a minute later. "I don't want to hide behind the comfortable spectacle of art, giving the audience an easy way out through catharsis, giving ourselves an easy way out through conscientious detachment. The audience's emotions are purged; they walk away feeling cleansed and enlightened. Our egos are boosted by the success of our creation; we walk away feeling virtuous and admired. But is that the point of what we're trying to do here? To help people feel cleansed and virtuous and detached? Isn't it more important now, in this moment and time, for us to feel dirty and compromised and complicit?" I had worked myself into a state and my body was visibly shaking. I saw a throw blanket held out before me, and I wrapped it around myself.

"I think it's safe to say that our goal isn't to create an easy way out for the audience," someone finally said, looking out on a circle of nodding heads. "After all, we've spent most of our career pushing the boundary between comfort and discomfort. Just look at the response to our work—half our listeners find our music beautiful, the other half find it grating and insufferable.

As a band, we have a love-hate relationship with our source materials. The automobile has propelled us to the place where we're at today. But is this where any of us wanted to end up?"

We all hung our heads in remorse—but I still needed more from them. "I have an idea. It's only a start and a crude one at that," I said after some time, looking up to see if anyone would balk at my opening. When no one did, I gathered up the courage to continue. "I think we have an opportunity here to take our audience through a scene of extremity. We can construct this scene however we like. But to keep things fair, to ward off our own detachment, we must be prepared to put ourselves on the line. We must be willing to personally undergo the torture that you have in mind."

The speaker looked to each band member for a moment before responding: "It's a tall order. But if that's what you think is needed for this project, then you can count us in." His words were uttered in a declarative tone that bespoke confidence, but also suggested, at least to my vigilant senses, the raising of a brave front. I didn't question their commitment further, but my feelings turned again—as they did so often in those days—to worry and fear.

RH: I'm sorry to stop us here, but I'm getting a signal that we need to break for station identification. [*Forty-five seconds of radio announcements*] We're back. First, I want to say it's been an immense pleasure talking with you. During the break, you talked a little about your working process. Can you elaborate on this for our listeners?

D: Of course. Like I said, I wish I could paint you a picture of us collaborating over several months—theorizing, debating, acting out various parts, going over potential soundtracks—but in truth our time together was terribly sporadic. After our initial meeting, we didn't speak again until just two and a half weeks before the scheduled performance. I know that sounds sloppy and haphazard but it wasn't really, considering all the weeks we had on our own beforehand to think about where we wanted to take our collaboration. So by the time we convened at the open lot for our first meeting on set, all the ideas that had been gestating in us came pouring out, and we were pleased and a little surprised to discover that we were thinking along the same lines.

In the meantime, the Ambient Parkers had persuaded some of the other dancers from my circle to join in similar collaborations, directing them to "forge anatomical expressions of twenty-first-century reality." On any given day, you could find the band holding court over the lot of the abandoned manufacturing plant that they had appropriated for their diabolical use, weaving in and out of makeshift scenes with handheld mikes, as my colleagues grimaced and writhed in rehearsal. It was really a sight to behold, and it attracted a dedicated following along with regular police patrols on those awful human transporters, who would observe the proceedings from an intrusive spot and ask a few probing questions, but ultimately glide away without incident.

In my time off set, I immersed myself in their music. I sat on a floor cushion and listened to their obscure releases and bootleg recordings, searching my own memories of their shows for some insight into their sound, some way to crack the enigma of their diesel sonatas. For days, my room reverberated with the noise of pounding engines and jangling guitars.

RH: Did you enjoy the experience?

D: [*Laughs*] I don't know how to answer that. It wouldn't be honest for me to say that I liked their songs or that their harmonies appealed to me. All I know is that I felt obligated to sit through the jarring noise and remain present, drastically present, till the very end. As the music blared out from the speakers, I wondered how anyone could possibly listen to it for fun.

At the time, the Ambient Parkers had a small but respectable following composed mainly of other artists, people who danced to their music and even found a sort of beauty in it, who felt that it spoke directly to them about their lives. They were all people a little bit younger than the band. [*Shifts in her chair*] I happen to believe that popular culture is defined by the big ongoing conversation between people who are a certain age and people who are a little bit younger—not just chronological age, but the conditions or sensibilities associated with being of a certain age. It's only a slight variance in years, but it makes all the difference. The artists who are a little bit older have a slight head start. They come onto the scene first and the freshness of their productions seems to capture the imagination of their younger audience. Everyone is pleased with themselves, feeling like they are standing knee-deep in the present moment, soaking up the zeitgeist. But there's something more going on here. The artists may think they're transmitting the present moment, but in reality their productions are always already dated and the best they can do is transmit the intentions of the past. Likewise, the listeners may think they are hearing a production of the present, when really they are the ones standing a few steps ahead; they are the ones who, by leaning into the performance and listening with the full force of their being, manage to transmit the intentions of the future. This is the conversation that unfolds between the generations, and we're always picking up new strands of it before we've exhausted the old ones. Time overlaps itself through productions of art; we all belong to the generation of the overlap.

At any rate, I could hear this overlap in their music. And from what I remember of their shows, others in the audience could hear it too, despite everyone's efforts to look away and pretend they hadn't heard what they'd so obviously just experienced.

There was a moment of awkwardness as each of us grappled with this new development—you could see it in the eyes of the musicians who struggled to maintain a sense of timing, in the faces of the spectators who swayed uncertainly, and in the confusion of the hard-core fans who tapped their foam earplugs and jerked their heads sharply to the side, as if they had just heard the same passage played twice, which of course they had. We all heard it twice, loud and clear: once for the transmission of the chord, and once again for its echo.

RH: Earlier, you mentioned that you met with the Ambient Parkers in the lot of an abandoned manufacturing plant. I'm curious, what was manufactured there?

D: Let me think. Oh yes, now I remember: metal keys for typewriters and adding machines. You could still see the faded paint lines in the cement lot, which had marked the parking spots for legions of workers who had once marched up the entrance ramp to the factory every morning. Now, they simply delineated different areas of the Ambient Parkers' stage—their vast, open stage with no true front or back, no curtain that could be drawn at the end of the performance. With a breeze blowing across the scrub grass pushing up through the wide cracks in its surface, the stage was open to sky and time, and it was strangely peaceful to be sitting there in the middle of it, slumped back in a folding chair or balanced on the chassis of one of the half-stripped vehicular monstrosities that the band had hauled in from the junkyard.

When I got there at last, after two bus transfers and a long ride down a deserted frontage road which the driver described as a continuous crime scene after dark, the whole ensemble was on break, their bodies draped over the grisly-looking cars, basking in the spring warmth. The band had gone off in search of pizza, and I took advantage of their absence to ask about the props, how it was possible for these hunks of metal to escape being detected and confiscated by the authorities. My friends just blinked at me lazily, but a nervous, excitable guy who I'd never seen before slid down from his perch and began talking into my face. Immediately I was overwhelmed by a wave of dislike for this person, or perhaps it was just the tepid gusts of bad breath coming from his mouth as he discoursed freely, eager to display his particular font of knowledge. As a rule, I distrust know-it-alls, but after a minute I actually found myself paying attention.

"The principle of concealment is relative, don't you think?" he said, or rather exhaled into my personal space. "These wrecks have lost their charm and mobility. But as Robert Smithson once alleged, they accrue monumental status through the workings of time and obsolescence. In another year or two, the seedlings and sedge will reclaim them completely. Meanwhile, the cumulative weight of their ruin serves as a form of camouflage against the landscape, causing them to melt into the earth seamlessly."

"Surely someone is bound to notice something," I countered, taking issue with these statements.

"Never mind about that," he said quickly before I could continue. "Haven't you ever noticed that the most pronounced quality of an occupied parking lot is absence? The more cars there are, the greater the absence. It's common knowledge, you can hide anything you want in a parking lot."

I stared at him blankly, not sure what to make of his claim. But later on, in private, it struck me as a perfect metaphor for the Ambient Parkers' music.

RH: Did you meet with the Ambient Parkers that day?

D: I did. The band returned empty-handed to the grumblings of everyone around me, who straggled off in pairs toward a dingy strip of fast-food restaurants and convenience stores. I greeted the musicians with a sweeping wave and they strolled toward me casually, careful to hide their excitement.

I read them excerpts from my notebook and demonstrated a few experimental choreographies. In return, they played me a few potential soundtracks and led me over to a crushed vehicle, inviting me to crawl inside. I squeezed into its disfigured interior, clambering over the gnarled pieces of metal and plastic, the mangled straps of safety belts. I carefully examined the headroom and legroom, as well as the sightlines to the outside world. Finally I wriggled out, stepped into the circle of faces that were fixed upon my every move with nervous anticipation, and voiced my approval. On my way past the head of the chassis, I chanced upon a piece of shiny painted metal, the lone remnant of the hood. "Cutlass Ciera?" I inquired, running my fingers across the taupe curve. "Dodge Dart," someone replied with a smile.

After lunch with the others, we began choreographing the dance. At first they were timid, perhaps reluctant to push me out of what they perceived to be my comfort zone. We were still getting to know one another, after all. But seeing as we were bound to get nowhere fast with such neurotic politeness, I began to prod and fluster them. I wrapped my body around hunks of metal and watched them flinch; then I repeated the move with slight variations. They saw themselves as benign interpreters of their contemporary environment, but I wanted to put them in touch with their dark side. I wanted them to acknowledge their underlying wickedness and embrace it, because as you know, you have to be a little wicked to carry off this kind of art. After some initial hesitation, they loosened up. They began feeding me directions cautiously, and then more deliberately as they grew more sure of themselves and their methods. They would encourage me to twist my arms a certain way or draw my knees in tight so that I would appear engulfed by the cagelike machine. Eventually, the power went to their heads and they began to operate from a rush of violent passion, which was exactly what the project required. They would command me to brush up against shards of glass or razor-sharp edges of plastic, pushing us all dangerously close to the exposed materials. "Further to the right!" they would cry. "Slower! More excruciating!"

I always complied; I never questioned their orders. There they were like little stage directors, little auteurs, waving their arms wildly and barking orders. And there I was obedient as a mouse, carrying out all their commands without complaint. Of course, my submission was a snare. It was a deliberate act of provocation engineered to lure them to the brink. They remained blissfully ignorant of our work's meaning until nearly the end, so intoxicated were they by the sheer elixir of power. The moment of understanding hit them on the last day of rehearsal, just as we were putting the finishing touches on my final moves, syncing up the soundtrack with my rasping breath and the patter of my fingertips across the glowing cell phone. They were switching routinely between tracks, fiddling with the bass levels and adjusting the fade-outs, when the meaning of our performance dawned on them at last and their faces darkened.

Have you ever seen a building lift and fall at once? They lifted their heads, but it was their faces that fell, their faces that collapsed with the force of their comprehension. Everything they had taken for granted, everything they had believed in up till that moment, was revealed to be nothing but edifice. Now that the edifice had crumbled, the only thing left for them was the scaffolding of pure conceit, and behind it, the stunned, frightened gaze of innocent corroborators who could never have imagined an experience quite like this one, who could never have foreseen the possibility of leaping straight from art to reality in quite this way. [*Pauses*]

It was a time when I was first experimenting with my repertoire and flying, you might say, by the seat of my pants. I tried out some of my signature moves for the first time in that wrecked vehicle—moves that I've since refined and perfected in more mature choreographies. But what I remember most about the performance—aside from the shivering of my frozen body and the palpable tension of the audience as they murmured and coughed and circled the stage—was just how far we strayed from our agreed-upon plan. The band had assembled an ambient soundtrack to accompany every one of my moves. But at the very last moment, they substituted a blank cassette tape in its place, which they flipped over every forty-five minutes with grim fidelity. For my part, I had devised an intricate three-and-a-half-hour choreography. But in conspiracy with the audience who seemed loath to have the dance end so soon, I improvised longer sets and stretched my performance out to nearly twelve hours. It was as if the only way we could go on was to rebel against our original program, the only way we could survive our experiment was to make the experiment itself too torturous to reproduce.

RH: What happened after the performance?

D: The stage was struck and the audience dispersed. All of us dancers and musicians just stood around in the eerie silence, incapable of consoling one another. Finally, we managed to caravan up the frontage road to an all-night diner where we sat, poking at plates of eggs and potatoes, struggling to put our thoughts in order.

It's been said that their work with the band, and my performance in particular, succeeded in radicalizing the dancers as a troupe. From that point on, they could no longer carry out a full-length choreography without making references to some larger ideological concern. That's certainly the impression you get if you follow their later movements—their residency in Central Europe, their extended investigations of Asia and Africa, their pilgrimage to the Middle East. I toured with them from time to time, but I functioned strictly as a guest performer, never as a true member of the troupe. This tacit arrangement was to my liking. The ordeal in the parking lot had affected me in a profoundly solo direction, and I had no choice but to follow the lonely path that had been revealed to me.

As for the Ambient Parkers, I really don't know what to say. Had I pushed them too far? Did they come to resent our time together? I could only watch with a pang of disappointment as they avoided my eyes and withdrew to the shelter of their unstable, creative thoughts. After the long ghostly night that ended with a collective loss for words, I discovered that my legs were immobilized by muscle cramps. It was up to the dancers to support me at each arm, guiding me slowly right foot over left, left foot over right, out through the doors of the diner and into the stinging light of dawn. They eased me into the back of a taxi, which ferried us up and over the hills, around the barricaded corridors of finance and commerce, and through a slalom course of flashing traffic lights to our co-op. With their arms interlocked in a firemen's lift, they managed to carry me up the two flights of rickety stairs to my bedroom. Fixed in their seats at the diner table, the Ambient Parkers were spared from witnessing my impending decline.

RH: How long did it take before you were able to dance again?

D: A lot longer than I expected. [*Sighs*] When I got home, I was overcome by tremendous exhaustion and then tremendous pain. I lay in bed the whole first week, succumbing to the fallout of my dance. The pain somehow grew, surging through my body like bad blood. It was relentless and unforgiving—throbbing in my head, convulsing up and down my spine, jolting me with a vicious jab in the ribs, swelling in the pit of my stomach. It stayed with me day and night like a constant companion—steady and unshakable.

I would have been lost beyond all reckoning if it hadn't been for Emi and Audrey, the two friends who came to look after me, bringing me apple juice and tomato soup. I watched with gratitude as they fluffed up my pillows, straightened up the papers I was too weak to put away myself, and folded up the clothes I had neglected in my convalescence. They entertained me with the latest gossip in the art world, and when my ears could withstand it, they played my favorite records at a soft volume on my old turntable. At times I asked them to read books to me, and they acted out the various roles, adopting a faux British accent for the narrator and adjusting their tone to match the moods of the different characters in dialogue. Their productions breathed life into my ravaged body, and before too long my pain began to fade.

By any standard, however, I was still in a bad way. To help speed my recovery, we devised a daily routine of physical therapy. With my friends supporting me on either side, I made slow steps around the perimeter of my room. Each laborious circuit of this track would bring me past my bookshelf with its melancholic array of half-read books, framed snapshots, and childhood mementos, all coated with a thick and impenetrable layer of dust. My thoughts would inevitably turn to the subject of failure, so that I forgot all about my prickling legs which seemed to have fallen asleep indefinitely.

One day as they led me around the sickroom, my friends fell into conversation about a new favorite author, whom they each had discovered by chance. This writer had been a journalist at one time and a nightclub operator after that, but it was his fiction that had brought him international acclaim, though only posthumously, for his manuscripts had languished unread in the lower compartment of a bank vault until they were exhumed three days after his death by a favorite grandniece, brought to the attention of the literary authorities, and subsequently published and translated into all the major languages. Being new to this author's life and work, I listened to my friends' exchange with interest.

"I was surprised by *Postcard from Purgatory*. Reading it was like stepping into a bath filled with toxic waste, extracting myself with great difficulty, and then finding that my body had mutated into a splendid vessel of art," Emi declared, tightening her grip around my waist.

"Talk about a page turner," Audrey said, as she matched her steps to mine. "I read it in a single sitting, nine hours straight at a café. I was unemployed then, so time was no object. I had three cups of coffee, two salads, a coconut macaroon, and then a glass of Riesling, which I savored slowly over the final chapter. Toward the end, I could no longer distinguish between my emotional life and the characters in the story. When Paolo finally broke down and wept, I felt like buying a copy of the book for everyone I knew. I rose from my seat feeling heroic. As I stepped onto the sidewalk, two people hailing the same cab happened to raise their arms in my direction, amounting to a public salute."

"When I first opened the book," Emi said, "I was dismayed to find the pages filled with hookers and hit men. I thought that I had fallen into the grip of yet another macho writer, another laureate of letters who's really a misogynist at the core. But I kept on reading—it was the only book I had with me at the time—and was relieved. No one is exempt from his penetrating gaze. He chronicles the exploitation of men and women alike, and the light he shines on his subjects is humane and equalizing."

"Most of his writing is profane," Audrey added. "I wouldn't excuse him from some untoward motive. Forbidden fruit, perhaps."

"You're right, the profanity is everywhere," Emi agreed. "It occupies the world of his characters like an infection, or more like a regional affliction that can be diagnosed, but never cured."

"I don't think any of his characters comprehend the nature of evil," Audrey continued after a moment. "It's what makes them sympathetic, but it also seals their fate. They are born into a corrupt world where they are compromised and exploited. They are compelled to commit crimes—thoughtless, senseless crimes—from which they are unable to extricate themselves."

"I feel both lost and affirmed by his writing," Emi said shortly after. "In the absence of a god, his characters stumble about blindly. They have nothing but their immediate world to depend on. And yet they still must come to terms with their lives, decide in which ways they are personally responsible. Most avoid this responsibility, but those who don't, like Paolo, are saved in the end."

"Paolo is definitely pushed beyond endurance," Audrey chimed in. "He must come to terms with the lonely conditions of his life and the whole wretched business of mortality."

She would have said more, but at that moment my strength gave out and my legs crumpled beneath me. The sudden drag of my dead weight caught my friends off guard, and we collapsed together in a heap on the floor. I couldn't help myself. I burst out laughing, and then just as my friends recovered their senses and began to perceive the comedy of our plight, I broke into tears. Something inside me just shattered, and I cried together with my friends like that, grievously and uncontrollably, for what seemed like a very long time.

RH: [*Pauses*] I'm getting another signal that we need to break. Why don't we stop here? [*Forty-five seconds of radio announcements*] We're back. Before moving on, let me just say that I appreciate you revealing this side of your work. I remember seeing some performance art in the 1970s, but I didn't know any of the artists personally. Do you normally experience this kind of fallout?

D: It's hard to say what's normal for me, but I do know that this time was entirely different. Over the weeks that followed, my condition slowly improved. I graduated to solid food and trained myself to walk again without support. Eventually, I grew strong enough to venture out from the co-op for a few hours at the start and end of each day, stealthy and crepuscular as a cat.

Outside, I encountered a world out of whack. It was as if I was looking at a picture on the wall knocked off balance, its corners at odd angles, its contents intact but hanging by a single frayed thread. I kept to the quieter thoroughfares and side streets, but even there the disturbance was palpable. People moved about with aggressive strides, throwing furtive glances in my direction or avoiding eye contact altogether. Whenever I did intersect the gaze of a stranger, I saw a look of desperate appeal, as if I were being asked to awaken the dead.

Occasionally, I searched for a place where I could sit down for a meal, but even the act of eating had become alienating. One afternoon at a downtown shopping mall, I followed a family of tourists to an underground food court. Taking the escalator, I descended into a coliseum of restaurant stalls purveying made-to-order dishes of every conceivable cuisine known to urban man. Cooks in starched aprons chopped, diced, seasoned, stir-fried, and grilled their designated foodstuffs, served up on disposable plateware that could be tossed at meal's end, or more often midmeal as soon as the diner grew bored with the entree and turned to the prospect of dessert. At the center of this arena, I saw what could only be described as a factory of industrious human jaws—chomping, smacking, slurping, swilling, and swallowing the spoils of the moment. All of the world's hunger was contained in those mouths, gnashing and tearing at the soft tissues of my being. The sights and sounds turned my stomach. I fled through the first fire exit that came into view and emerged onto an alleyway occupied by a miserable population of homeless humanity, their hats passively inverted to solicit spare change.

I turned to the world of nature, but my encounters with the animal population brought me no solace. Pigeons, some with eye growths or a missing foot, pecked at the sparkling concrete and asphalt, blowing a few feet away whenever they were hit by a rush of pedestrians or cars. Squirrels stood up on their haunches and gazed vigilantly into the distance, awaiting their frenzied moment to scour the garbage cans. Dogs at the ends of short leads were yanked away from petting hands and tempting smells. Even the insects were ravenous in their own way.

RH: Did these experiences drive you deeper inside your art?

D: When my thoughts turned to my last performance, I felt terribly wronged and wanted to hold someone responsible. For a long time afterward, resentment welled up in me and I needed to direct it at someone—the band or the audience—anyone who had stood by in a cloak of innocence as I died by slow degrees.

I resumed my dancing as soon as I could. I practiced yoga twice a day to get back into shape. I began work on a few new choreographies, with little success. My physical strength had returned, but the real life had gone out of my body. When I danced, I could achieve only wooden movements and hollow gestures. I would manage to strike a technical pose, but only by lifting and placing my limbs mechanically, as if I were a large doll or marionette. Maybe I'll become a puppeteer, I thought to myself bitterly.

In the weeks that followed, the local climate oscillated between extremes of hot and cold, driven by mysterious pressures in the upper atmosphere. One morning, a storm touched down from the northern Pacific, dumping rain and hail on unsuspecting residents. It was a chilly, wet day, the kind of day that draws you into deep retreat or out into the great silver expanse, into the clouds of mercurial air, into the swift outpour of the streets, all in a quest to reach the ideal public interior, to feed the desire to be at once alone and not alone—stamping your feet at the threshold of a welcoming pub, nursing a pot of tea in a familiar café, browsing the aisles of a record store amidst a crowd of like-minded strangers.

This was the native impulse that drove me out of the co-op and over to the nearest intersection, where I boarded a soggy, heaving bus that transported me across town to the steps of the main public library. There was nothing I wanted more that day than to lose myself in the gliding shelves of books, the ones arranged like massive accordion pleats that open or collapse with the turn of a crank. I wandered through the collections, weaving in and out of the new fiction section, reference section, sheet music and oversized folio section, planting myself at last in a squat armchair beneath a capacious skylight. I looked out to see similar squat armchairs arranged at casual intervals and occupied by a patchwork community of readers, to which I now added my own person. I sorted through the pile of books that I had plucked from the shelves and placed them atop the arm of my reading chair like a protective wall.

I became immersed in the activity of reading, the luxury of being in a warm, dry place as the rain drummed against the convex surface of the domed skylight. I turned the pages of my book steadily, grazing upon the words and pictures trailing off into the margins. Between chapters, I would glance over at the slanted cone of silvery light pooling down from the sky onto the library floor, and I would allow my eyes to rest there as I thought how much it resembled an effusion of sunlight in a forest. And just as sunlight in a forest, however bright and dazzling, does not attain its full meaning until some wild creature scampers or trots noiselessly into the glow and pauses there midmotion to complete it, so the light pooling down from the sky onto the library floor was remarkable but unfinished, for there was something missing from it, something vital and animating that did not fully enter the picture until I looked up from my book to see Jerrod Jaggabatara standing there in the light.

He was wearing his signature uniform of white T-shirt and blue jeans, his hands in his pockets, his elaborately painted arms naked to the biceps. He was looking up at the circle of sky with his back turned toward me, soaking in the radiance, drinking in the flow of raindrops that streamed down and landed on the outside of the dome. As the storm resurged, the raindrops drummed against the surface with such forceful rebound that they seemed to fall back up into the sky, as if impelled to do so by the sheer intensity of Jerrod's gaze. I adjusted my position in the chair, leaning forward to get a better look at the light that Jerrod was now blocking with his shoulder. But perhaps it isn't quite right to say this—that his presence caused the room to darken—because in actuality the opposite was true. In the emotional sense, Jerrod was a beacon and he generated his own light. There was a brightness about him that I had always been aware of, at first dimly when he began to appear in the general purview of my casual friends and then more distinctly when I volunteered to sit for one of his designs. He slung his messenger bag off his shoulder, shedding the light at my feet like so many tiny pools of illumination. I felt profound relief followed by profound loss, as I realized just how much had been missing from my life before now.

He turned around to face me and smiled, for he had apparently been aware of my presence far longer than I had been of his. After greeting one another, we began to talk about ourselves and the people we shared in common—not gossip, but merely a curious exchange of news and tidbits with no malicious subtext. As we talked, I saw that the essence of Jerrod's brightness originated not from his skin, which in spite of its rich undertones and varicolored designs exhibited no special incandescence, nor from any superficial bluster in his personality. His presence was solid in a subtle, masculine way, finding expression not through swag and banter but through a quiet sense of command—for why should he thrust himself forward in a crowd when he could simply anchor himself and wait for others to be drawn to the magnetic core of his being? As we stood under the skylight a few feet apart, just looking at each other and talking in an easy, unpretentious way, it suddenly struck me that this was the true origin of his brightness, this exceedingly open and candid way of being. Others in my place might have felt overwhelmed, as if too much illumination was being thrown onto their lives, to which they would have preferred to remain ignorant. But I preferred knowledge, and that's why I let the pile of books slide down to the floor behind me when I stood up to just exist awhile in Jerrod's presence, in the frank simplicity of our talk which amounted to a kind of understanding, a willingness to be fully engaged and present with one another, to be quietly extraordinary.

RH: It sounds like this meeting was a turning point for you.

D: Yes, very much so. [*Pauses*] It seemed only natural that our talk should turn, after a few exchanges, to the subject of my unfinished design. And it was only to be expected that, after a preliminary inspection of the inky abstractions on my shoulder, we should arrive at an agreement to finish the work at once. After stopping at the counter to check out our books—a collection of Lorenzo Thomas poems for him, an illustrated field guide to local birds for me—we exited the library together. We took long strides across oily puddles and minor whirlpools, trudging through a half-dozen intersections until we reached the outer threshold of the gallery, where we paused to shake the rain out of our umbrellas.

We pushed open the door to enter a dry, spacious room with a crackling hearth fire, which turned out to be not an actual fire at all but the looping video footage of one on a television monitor. A very small boy sat cross-legged on a shag rug before the screen, scribbling in a coloring book while his father considered the black-and-white photographs of melting glaciers affixed to the gallery walls. The man paused before each image, raising his finger from time to time at the young gallery assistant seated behind the reception desk, who immediately made a note in her ledger. During these operations, she must have exchanged some silent signal with Jerrod, for a piece of the rear gallery wall suddenly swung open like a secret door in a spy movie. We waited, dripping helplessly onto the floor, until an adolescent in her mid-forties emerged from the doorway and tossed us each a freshly laundered towel. Once we had dried off to her liking, she collected the damp towels and motioned for us to accompany her. Like characters from a distant dream, the gallery assistant and her client looked up absently as we swept past them.

I followed Jerrod and our guide into a dim corridor lined with framed photographs and business certificates. The passageway narrowed as we progressed, sloping sharply downward and veering to the left, as if we were inside a tunnel that had been bored through the foundation of the building. The void was interrupted only by a vague light glimmering ahead of us, the silence broken only by the rhythmic clinking of our guide's pendulous body jewelry. At last we reached a green velvet curtain, which our guide drew open with practiced authority. We found ourselves in a small alcove surrounded by faux wood paneling and decorated with strings of Christmas lights suspended from finger hooks. The curtain swished closed behind us as our guide withdrew.

Jerrod led me into a room noisy with buzzing needles, past the prostrate clients splayed out on makeshift operating tables in various stages of inscription, and all the way back to one of the recessed stations, where a large swing-armed lamp rested next to an old-fashioned secretary desk and a padded stool mounted on casters. He switched on the lamp, rolled the stool aside, pulled up a small cushioned armchair for me, and then stepped over to a pedestal sink to scrub his hands. He ran the water hot, lathering the soap briskly between his palms and onto his forearms.

Under the harsh lamplight, Jerrod's brightness was still evident but muted, and he seemed to withdraw into himself. I watched as he plunged his hands into the water, his eyes staring straight into the swirl of steam, his jaw clenching then softening, his expression darkening then lightening. And I saw for the first time that there was something broken about him, something wounded yet resilient, some visible trace of sorrow that he had to overcome to be bright. I now watched him with new admiration, for I recognized how I lacked the strength of character and inner resources to generate my own light. So far, I could only stumble about in the shadows, groping for the nearest supports and footholds, pushing my body to perform by sheer will. Perhaps I was nothing more than a pusher, exerting myself continually but going nowhere. Wasn't my dancing just another pusher activity, a way of feeding personal ambition and group mania?

At last Jerrod shut off the tap and patted his arms dry with a clean towel. Planting himself on the stool and scooting up beside me, he scrutinized the half-drawn shapes on my shoulder. He frowned, evidently worried about his ability to bring the design to completion. "The person is missing," I thought I heard him mutter. But when asked to repeat, he simply said, "There's a piece missing here." Then, as if remembering me, he straightened up and gave me a reassuring smile. He seized the needle gun and set straight to work.

The first jab punctured my skin, setting my right shoulder on fire. Tiny jets of ink shot under my skin as the electric needle buzzed and vibrated. The design would have to be worked from the inside out, starting from the dead center and moving to the outer edges in overlapping passes. Through the blur of pain, I eased into the rhythm and pace of Jerrod's work. He stepped back from time to time to survey his progress and consult with me, but for the most part he stayed hunched over my shoulder, murmuring so softly that it took a full minute before I registered that his words were meant for me.

"I wasn't planning on telling you this," he said, glancing away momentarily to check the ink supply, "but I spotted you around town a number of times after your last performance. You were always alone, looking visibly distracted or upset. I sensed how much you valued your anonymity, so I didn't approach you. You never noticed me, did you?"

I told him I never did.

"One time I saw you in the museum of modern art, at the big anniversary show," he continued. "You were moving slowly through the galleries and I decided to follow behind at a discreet distance. You spent a lot of time in the room with the giant vertical paintings, the ones like sheets of glazed glass."

"I remember," I said. "The artist had laid each canvas out on the floor of her studio. She pulverized various rocks and minerals that she had found in the desert and smeared the powdery residue across the canvas. Then she brushed on layers of resin, adding swaths of monochromatic paint between the layers. The results were amazing. Standing amongst them, I felt like I was in church—not a false church erected by the authorities, but one forged by unseen forces, lodged deep inside the earth's core."

"You stood for a long time under the yellow ocher canvas," he said, "the one with nickel scattered across it. I was about to walk away, but at the last moment something held me back and I stayed. A whole fleet of emotions was moving across your face. You looked doubtful and sorrowful, then solemn and transfixed. Now that I have you here, I can ask you: was that your idea of worship?"

He kept the needle dancing steadily on my shoulder, which had become a miniature trauma site, a field of localized agony. Suddenly I was hit with a wave of exhaustion. The air swam before me and a pair of blackout curtains appeared in the center of my vision. With all my strength, I pushed them back. I spoke through the fatigue and pain, articulating each word slowly and with great effort.

"For a long time," I said, "I thought that if I dedicated myself to dancing, I'd be able to get some grasp on the world, make it into an object that could be fixed and comprehended. But the more I stared at the canvas, the more uncertain I felt. The resin was thick and glossy, and I could see myself reflected in the surface. I felt like one of those flecks of nickel suspended inside the paint, trapped. Art has always been my solace. But am I fooling myself? Am I experiencing the world through a shiny veneer?"

I glanced over to catch Jerrod's reaction, but he was lost now in the depths of the design, eyes burning, brows furrowed. I thought: What am I waiting for, some kind of sign from him? Just once, I'd like someone to answer me, straight without flinching: What's the point of it all?

RH: [*Pauses*] Those are difficult questions, I know.

D: Yeah. [*Pauses*]

Jerrod was now working on the heart of the design, coloring in the gaps, tying critical pieces and elements together. The rain had stopped and an icy draft was blowing into the room from a wall vent. I gave in to the chill, my body sinking by slow degrees into a physical numbness that camouflaged my pain. And in that moment of freefall, I understood that I had never really left the car wreck at all. I was still wedged inside the twisted shell, my legs pinned together, a sharp splinter of metal digging into my shoulder. I was dancing, Jerrod's needle was dancing; we were performing a duet. I was trying to communicate something through each one of my movements. I could feel the pressure of the audience gathered outside, the open-mouthed awe of the musicians as they pointed their microphones at the wreck. *They are recording artists*, I thought, *but I am a performing artist.*

Jerrod lifted the needle and repositioned it on my skin. His face looked drawn. Perhaps, like me, he was tired of all the assumptions we had grown accustomed to living by. Perhaps he was tired of living in a world without standards, where it didn't seem to matter if things went one way or the other. So was that what we were trying to do here? To communicate a standard, to make the world matter again?

The musicians are probably still congregated around the wreck, peering inside its jagged openings, documenting the freakish silence with their studious machines. They strain to hear what they can't hear, to capture what they can't possibly capture. They are recording artists, but I am a performing artist. *So perform*, I commanded myself.

I threw my body into the choreography. My back tensed. My arm twitched involuntarily. I was sweating profusely, in spite of the draft. I thought of all the people I was dancing for, the ones surrounding the wreck and the countless others buried in the ground beneath it, all the people that I had ministered to and would leave behind in my selfish need to be an artist, to perform my art in spite of and for the sake of them. "Are you crying, Karen?" Jerrod asked, pressing my arm gently. And as he switched off the needle and pushed the terrible instrument away, as he sat beside me and looked into my face, I summoned up the last of my strength and lifted, god help me, I lifted myself out of the wreck.

THE VOICE ARTIST

After listening to the end of the dancer's interview, we exited
the park in a daze, following our dogs without thinking. As we
wandered the streets, we recalled our impression of the dancer
from our collaboration and compared it with her radio presence.
The quiet, pensive girl whom we remembered from rehearsal had
been a mystery to us, performing her drastic movements without
complaint and eyeing us from time to time with fascination and
concern. Now, after hearing her on-air testimony, we understood
that she had been watching us for a very long time—watching
us patiently from a close distance without speaking.

Meanwhile, the commute hour had arrived and traffic swelled.
We ambled along the sidewalk as our dogs nosed ahead, barking
at the unfriendly vehicles with their menacing tires and stinking
trails of exhaust. As the boulevards widened, the automobiles
gathered in force, broadcasting their motorized messages—
flashing brake lights, pulsing turn signals, blaring horns. In this
mechanized environment, it was the people who were outmoded
and forgotten, their voices replaced by the crude exchange of
their transport.

We slunk home and sat quietly in the half-darkness, watching
the curtains flutter before our open window. Midnight found us
in a state of agitation, our bodies trembling. A single refrain

occupied our thoughts: we had failed to record the dancer's voice in the wrecked automobile. Unable to console one another, we vowed to change our music, to further represent the unspoken by making an audible dent in the world with our voices.

The next morning, we drove our bus to the roof level of a downtown garage, cut the motor, and opened the doors for optimal acoustics. Listening to the noise of city traffic, we took up the recumbent positions of passengers and raised our pens tentatively, scribbling the first of our lyrics in pocket-sized notebooks. As time passed, we came to look less like a band than a caravan of struggling poets, our eyes fixed on random points in the distance, our fingers running perpetually through our forelocks.

With shy exhilaration, we returned to the loft and dusted off our karaoke machine. To exercise our upper registers, we set its playlist to a medley of early Motown hits and nudged the pitch control ever higher. Pleased with our singing range, we sat at the keyboard and tried our hand at composition, fitting our experimental vocals to the bass-line riffs in our recordings. At last we took turns occupying the shower stall for its surround sound and delivered the words to our songs, as our manager listened appraisingly.

Initially, our manager encouraged our efforts with benevolent smiles and measured praise. But later he took to wearing plaid woolen earmuffs and fleeing the premises during our a cappella rehearsals. After many such occurrences, we found a sheet of his monogrammed letterhead slipped beneath the bathroom door. Halting an impromptu concert, we read what appeared to be the copy for an on-line ad:

Quasi-environmental, post-rock band seeks experienced vocalist to help drive its ensemble. Male or female voice okay. All genres and styles of singing welcome. Must be open to collaborative improvisation, duets with inanimate objects, and sonic extremes. Songwriting skills a plus. We have released two EPs and one full-length album, and are ready to take our music to the next level. Interviews and auditions on the third, fifth, and eighth of the month. Send voice samples, along with a brief description of your background and influences, to Box #9264753.

Sobered by our manager's disfavor, we set aside our pop aspirations and embarked on the search for a singer. The prospect of a new band member filled us with excitement and uncertainty. We screened the initial pool of applicants, rejecting most out of hand and admitting a total of eight to the next round. In the second cut, we eliminated three candidates for poor auditions and two more for irreconcilable aesthetic differences. This left us with three remaining contenders, all comparable in skill and experience, despite their contrasting styles and philosophies. For the final round, we summoned each to our studio and tested their mettle with an extended jam session.

The first finalist was a fastidious perfectionist and self-described ethnomusicologist. Gesturing with his hands in upward sweeps, he insisted that we quicken our tempos to accommodate his exacting mélange of down-home roadside rap and cockney rhyming slang. In a concluding solo, he surprised us all by shifting to a slow, plaintive melody, his woebegone crooning reminiscent of a children's lullaby.

The second finalist impressed several of us by arriving with a collection of songs that she had written specially for the occasion. Dissonant and thought-provoking, the lyrics took after "Ambient Parking #25" in mood and the poems of Barbara Guest in form. After delivering a poignant finale in modern hexameter, she stayed on for drinks and shared the fundamentals of her musical poetics with us over a leisurely bottle of grappa.

The third finalist was by far our favorite, despite his unstable ways. He arrived forty minutes late in a dull stupor suggestive of habitual inebriation and proceeded onto the stage in an off-putting manner. Yet our repulsion was instantly dispelled by the beauty of his singing, which spanned three blissful octaves and pushed the envelope of expressive genius. With his half-closed eyes and jagged, liquid mouth, his spiky hair and sudden jackknifing body, he looked less like a human being than a ravening bird, a feral, loveless monster hatching out from the cracked macadam shell of our music. He sang for nearly an hour, and then draped himself over the amplifier and passed out cold. In ecstatic whispers, we discussed plans for his future while he snoozed and snored.

Our debut performance together was a mixed bill of elation and disaster. We opened with a long set of atmospheric progressions driven by wanderlust and a steady motorik beat. Over this rolling groundwork, our singer emitted sounds that were not quite words but an impression of language, not quite language but a gradual crescendo of lamentations that orbited the bass line for a dozen measures before climbing up to a tenor range of pure wailing. As he sang, something strange happened to his body. His chest broadened, his torso stretched to the sky, and a sublime glow appeared around his head. He became ferociously beautiful, and the audience soon learned to worship their new demigod of the stage.

The concertgoers gasped with speechless awe before bursting into violent applause. After two more instrumental numbers, it was time for a breather. During intermission, we caught a glimpse of our frontman surrounded by a bevy of female admirers who hung upon his every word and gazed up at him in star-struck wonder. When we glanced over a second time, we saw him draped over the bar like a deflated balloon. The girls had vanished and he was drinking alone, all his beauty and charisma gone.

His return to the stage was fitful and haphazard. He stared absently into the distance during our extended intro, missing his entrance on the thirty-second bar. After eight more bars of miscues, we ad-libbed backup vocals until he shook free from his trance and hummed along for the remainder of the song. His performance subsequently improved, and audience members who had walked out during the opening debacle slowly trickled back in. He managed to carry on with his singing part, a notable feat considering that he sang with his back to the audience for one song and delivered another solo while sprawled out on the floor. His incessant yawning, however, did not bode well for the closing act. A heavy drowsiness crept into his voice, and by the middle of the song he was lost in slumber. We covered his part with a mash-up of traffic noise and then carried him offstage before the silent contempt of our fans.

Against our better judgment, we retained him for another month, hoping to reprise his moments of onstage genius. We supplied him with smart drinks and barred his access to the bar, steering him away from all substances liable to cause enervation. Yet despite our best efforts, his brilliance never returned. There were occasional rays of hope, instances of divine intervention in which he channeled the unspoken, but such moments were sadly short-lived, eclipsed by the very next chorus or downbeat. Meanwhile, our relationship with him declined. He was chronically late for practice, spinning fantastic tales to excuse himself. At other times he appeared agitated and distraught, pulling one of us aside to reveal his conspiracy theories and woes.

Finally he left us altogether, disappearing after a particularly bad show with an entourage of cronies and a bottle of gin. Our relief was immediate and gratifying. Soon we began casting around for a replacement, littering on-line bulletin boards with want ads and scoping out open jam sessions for fresh talent. We dedicated our time to sifting through demo tracks and chasing down leads, but the perfect voice continued to elude us. No one, it seemed, could help us personalize our music.

To make matters worse, our manager had grown distracted and aloof ever since our singer's departure. In the mornings, he barely touched his toast and ducked behind the front-page headlines whenever we tried to greet him or engage him in light conversation. After breakfast he would jump up, snatch his coat and muffler, and hurry out the door to take, as he liked to put it, a long constitutional for the preservation of his sanity. Many hours passed before his return, whereupon he would collapse on the couch and cough up cryptic answers to our questions about business matters. In the absence of his direction, we had no choice but to take our career into our own hands, thumbing through office files and adopting a chipper professional demeanor in public.

One day after an exhausting interview with an overly enthusiastic singer-songwriter, we came home to find our manager decked out in a three-piece suit and brogues, pacing next to a mound of packed bags. He looked up sharply when we entered, visibly jolted. Extending an arm with nervous ceremony, he sat us down and revealed the momentous news: in the wake of his fiftieth birthday, it was time for him to move on. After much agonizing debate, he had decided to pursue a lucrative opportunity as the impresario for an up-and-coming boy band. Choking back sobs as he bade farewell to each one of us in turn, he scooped up his bags and rushed out the front door to meet a waiting taxi.

Weary and discouraged, we revisited our roots, journeying to the old garage structures that had fueled our initial creations. Some of the sites had been razed to the ground to make way for terraced apartments and shopping plazas, but most were as we remembered—a bit more car-worn and polluted perhaps, but still populated by scores of driverless vehicles that stunned us with their dread and vacant beauty. Heady from nostalgia and lingering fumes, we staggered past columns of numbered spaces, reaching out to slide our palms across gleaming hoods, dusty fenders, sidewalls of youthful, freewheeling escape now consigned to their individual resting spots. Were we destined to stay parked like this forever, to commune indefinitely with a faceless, pitiless field?

We drowned our despair in torrents of work. Taking up where our manager had left off, we pored over financial reports under unforgiving light and acquainted ourselves with the bottom line. Inevitably, we would walk past our recording studio and peek in at our guitars standing idle, beckoning to us with their polished curvatures and untuned strings. The challenge of finding a lead singer had stymied us and we were reluctant to resume our search. Instead, we decided to look among ourselves for someone to enhance our rehearsals, someone to function as if not a singer, then a temporary stand-in.

As we looked around the room, it occurred to us that one of our members hadn't participated in our earlier karaoke sessions and shower recitals. Seated on the floor in the back corner, she curled up into herself, blushing and trying to shield herself from notice. The shyest member of our band, she had always avoided the spotlight, while the greater society around her clamored for center stage. In her time away from her music, she could be found in the throes of a self-pedicure or, more often than not, behind the tattered cover of a classic novel, immersed in its romantic and revolutionary storylines. In our time on the road together, she would be the first to spot the animals enduring among us—a hawk hunting from the top of a signpost, a deer and her spotted fawn grazing on the grasses mere yards away from speeding cars, a raccoon darting across the road and down into the temporary shelter of a storm drain—and those who had failed to survive and now lay dead on the asphalt. While we averted our eyes, she would scoop up the bodies with her sweatshirt and carry them to the side of the road, placing them atop a bed of leaves or amidst the wildflowers. After these ceremonies, she would look at everything around her with a renewed sense of urgency.

We realized with a start that if there was one among us who could represent the unspoken, it was she—for in many ways she already had. We took her shyness into account, making no declarations of such, and invited her to be our stand-in vocalist. She looked up in surprise and then cast her eyes to the ground. With a trace of regret, she said that she was not a singer.

We gave her time to warm up to the idea and even brought home famous voice recordings for inspiration, but her answer was always the same. One evening after she had resisted our entreaties for weeks, we heard a series of faint sounds rising above the running water as she filled the bath. At last she was singing. We dared not say a word lest she stop altogether, until she had sung many times this way in the privacy of her bath. At our next practice session, we petitioned her once more. To our surprise, she took a deep breath before nodding her assent. With giddy excitement, we led her to the microphone stand and adjusted it to her height.

Just as we suspected, her voice was fundamentally flawed. It was thin and wispy, barely audible over our dense instrumentation. In her every inflection, she emanated a soft feminine grace that was incongruous with the machines. As the song advanced, she gathered determination, her breath quickening with the lead-in beat to every measure. She sighed, she sang, and she blundered, but most of all she struggled—straining against her vocal limitations, which were considerable. And when we saw how she tried again and again to reach moments of expression that were utterly beyond her, how her face looked stricken as she pleaded with the music for acceptance, we learned to forgive her. We forgave her flaws and missing gifts, and we began in that moment, through the faculties of sympathy and understanding, to forgive ourselves.

We rehearsed day and night, building our music up in segments as the automobiles droned steadily below our open window. We felt mysteriously compelled by her singing. Artless and unadorned, her voice had become if not quite beautiful, then starkly convincing to us.

Our concert premiere took place at noon on a grassy meridian strip just outside a bustling commercial zone. It was a sun-streaked day, full of sure optimism and the confidence of junior freelancers picnicking on the lawn with steaming bento boxes. The mood was youthful and bright. Encouraged by the scene, we set up stage in the middle of the strip, near a commemorative battle statue retrofitted with an assortment of community fliers and knit caps.

We sank into the opening chords with characteristic aplomb, launching our music into the heart of the crowd. The spectators chattered idly through our redundant intro. But when our vocalist entered, the talk died down and many faces lifted with interest. She sang with surprising warmth and personal feeling, drawing the audience in with her imperfect voice, pushing the song forward in spite of her faulty tunings. Humbled by her performance, we lowered our instruments and softened our ambient noise.

And now our siren moved up close to the microphone, singing earnestly into the languid air. She held her mouth open until the words reverberated and the refrain vanished into the back of her throat, an invocation sung internally. As the concert progressed, her mouth became a kind of cavern from which she projected an ancient noise, half-ruined and half-holy. Cars looped around us in sluggish circles; traffic took on the qualities of continental drift. We tried to recall the direction of our many recordings, the countless hours we'd spent in the shadow of parked sedans, but none of that seemed to matter now. Our heroine hummed, and the trucks slowed to a grinding halt. She caught her breath, and a luxury cab stalled. The asphalt resonated with the noise of failing machines.

After the concert, we gathered our equipment and headed homeward, taking side streets to avoid the crowds. As we emerged from a service alley and turned left, we stumbled upon a crumbling parking lot pitted with potholes and occupied by a single hoodless car. We blinked at the familiar ruin as though it were a memory from a distant dream.

Lying in our beds that night, we were unable to shake off the vision. We dreamt of propulsion and acceleration, ecstatic velocities made possible by fossil fuel and combustion. We could hear an engine roll over in place, gathering volume with each revolution until it turned into something monstrous and inhuman. It was tempting to lose ourselves inside its ambient roar, blotting out everything aside from sound and speed and thrumming air.

As the pane of glass lowered, the wind thrashed in our ears so urgently, obliging us to reject our soft-bodied selves in favor of sheer motion. Soon, there would be no difference between us and the road. We would be nothing but a smear below the horizon, the faintest memory of a speeding shadow.

Zooming past signposts and mile markers, we gunned the motor and sang at the top of our lungs, striving to reach the limit of absolute escape. Midsong, our voices broke off. We slowed to a crawl, veered off the shoulder, and puttered, after a series of lurches and bumps, to a dead stop. Stranded in the dark, stalled in a clearing somewhere off the beaten path, we had no choice but to stay put and listen. A vast and silent emptiness confronted us, filling our bones with dread.

A dim, road-weary part of us still recalled the voices of the living—all the warbling, caterwauling, and howling voices of the animals and their miraculous presence on earth—along with the murmuring roots, whispering crops, and rustling trees, their vital branches and stems and the insects that feasted on leaves at the ends of these stems, their tiny jaws clicking as they chomped on the soft-fibered green. Transported to a moment of grace, we wanted more than anything to take it home with us, tucked between the folds of our consciousness like a glimmer in the carbon black night, to be held, shielded, and sustained through the ghostly hours until morning.

We awoke the next day, wide-eyed and clearheaded, to the sounds of our unspectacular existence. First came the low whine of the street-sweeping tank, rasping the asphalt below our open window with its giant brushes. A station wagon chugged around the block, shooting out newspapers to land thud-heavy on neighboring porches. Buses pulled up the main drag, rattling hard on the incline before wheezing to a stop. We could hear the commuters off-boarding, the regular clip-clop of their heels as they headed to work.

Tan Lin's *Insomnia and the Aunt* is an ambient novel composed of black and white photographs, postcards, Google reverse searches, letters, appendices, an index to an imaginary novel, re-runs and footnotes. The aunt in question can't sleep. She runs a motel in the Pacific Northwest. She likes watching Conan O'Brien late at night. She may be the narrator's aunt or she may be an emanation of a TV set. Structured like everybody's scrapbook, and blending fiction with non-fictional events, *Insomnia and the Aunt* is about identities taken and given up, and about the passions of an immigrant life, rebroadcast as furniture. Ostensibly about a young man's disintegrating memory of his most fascinating relative, or potentially a conceptualist take on immigrant literature, it is probably just a treatment for a prime-time event that, because no one sleeps in motels, lasts into the late night and daytime slots. / ISBN: 978-0-9767364-7-9 / $10.00

Brian Massumi once wrote that the conscious narration of affective states is subtractive, a retrospective reduction of underlying bodily complexity made to fit requirements of continuity and linear causality. Sliding away from the "continuities" of foreclosed presents and enfolded pasts, **Jesse Seldess'** *Left Having* might be read as a *non*-subtractive exploration of the virtual remainders of such narrations (of historical trauma, of the time of events, of a person now present in a city or a room...). Seldess resituates us "Beyond the scattered signaling" of history – in pulse rates that flow through and across their own fractures and stalls – so we can hear the "Distance just now reaching us." These signalings (with gracefully decaying half tones in them) evoke both the familiarity and strangeness of durational life. As in the epigraph to the book taken from Alvin Lucier's famous work (in which he records his own "disfluent" speech, playing it back into the room and re-recording it repeatedly), what can finally be heard in Seldess' writing are the resonant frequencies of the architecture itself. That architecture's "End" (of which Seldess has also produced a video with artist Leonie Weber) is always ending but never done, because it turns back into itself (through us) toward something...else.—Laura Elrick / ISBN: 978-0-9767364-8-6 / $14.95

from Kenning Editions

Kevin Killian and David Brazil's *The Kenning Anthology of Poets Theater: 1945-1985* is wide-ranging, eclectic… Forces and influences are carefully and thoughtfully delineated, and a map of the progress of poets' theater in that crucial transition period between high modernism and post-modernism is brought into view.—Mac Wellman. The first anthology of its kind, *The Kenning Anthology of Poets Theater* includes work by Kathy Acker, John Ashbery, Russell Atkins, Steve Benson, Carla Harryman, Kenneth Koch, Michael McClure, Jackson Mac Low, Charles Olson, Ntozake Shange, Fiona Templeton, and many others in its nearly 600 pages, all copiously annotated. Also included are previously unpublished plays by Jack Spicer, V.R. "Bunny" Lang, James Schuyler, Robert Duncan, Madeline Gleason, Diane di Prima, Barbara Guest, James Keilty, Theresa Hak Kyung Cha, Johanna Drucker, and Nada Gordon. / ISBN: 978-0-9767364-5-5 / $25.95

Hannah Weiner's Open House, by Hannah Weiner, edited by Patrick F. Durgin. Hannah Weiner is one of the great American linguistic inventors of the last thirty years of the 20th century. Patrick Durgin has brought together touchstone works, some familiar and some never before published. *Hannah Weiner's Open House* provides the only single volume introduction to the full range of Weiner's vibrant, enthralling, and unique contribution to the poetry of the Americas.— Charles Bernstein / ISBN: 978-0-9767364-1-7 / $14.95

sexoPUROsexoVELOZ and Septiembre, **by Dolores Dorantes**, translated by Jen Hofer. Few poets these days are able to evoke and inhabit disquietude with the concentrated intensity of Mexican writer Dolores Dorantes, and this beautifully produced bilingual collection is powerful evidence of this. … (Translator Jen) Hofer is not only faithful to Dorantes' meticulous deployment of words, but also introduces a necessary defamiliarizing—one could say baroque—note into what remains for Latin Americans an imperial language, compelling monolingual North Americans to read differently and think differently about their language (which, in the end, is what poetry is all about).—Christopher Winks / ISBN: 978-0-9767364-2-4 / $14.95

Kenning Editions are distributed to individuals and the trade by Small Press Distribution / www.spdbooks.org / 800 869 7553. Discounts can be had by subscription and direct orders at www.kenningeditions.com.